MIDNIGHT TURNING GRAY

Midnight Turning Gray

Short Stories By
Peter Matthiessen

&

Ampersand Press
Roger Williams College
Bristol, RI 02809

Acknowledgment is made to the following publications in which these stories first appeared:

The Atlantic Monthly: "Sadie" and "The Fifth Day"

Harper's Bazaar: "The Wolves of Aquila"

Harper's Magazine: "Travelin Man"

New World Writing: "Late in the Season"

The Paris Review: "A Replacement"

"Midnight Turning Gray" is reprinted from *The Saturday Evening Post* ©1963 The Curtis Publishing Company.

Library of Congress Catalogue Card Number: 83-82381

ISBN 0-9604740-5-6

Midnight Turning Gray Copyright © 1984 by Peter Matthiessen

Composition by Coastal Composition
Box 2600, Ocean Bluff, MA 02065

Layout and design by Coastal Composition and Ampersand Press

Printed in U.S.A.

Published by Ampersand Press, Creative Writing Program,
Roger Williams College, Bristol, RI 02809

for Sherry

My friend for nearly fifty years—Good Lord!—who pestered me to return to fiction before the smoke clears.

CONTENTS

SADIE

Hell, it ain't that nigger boy beat Pentland to death, it's Dewey Floyd. One of these days he'll come back out of the swamp, and that stick right in his hand. The way that man looks at things, I reckon he'd as soon be strung up as not.

I was over in Cady last February to see about their dogs, which they say is the best in Georgia. I was told to see this Mister Pentland, and if he weren't there, a feller name of Dewey Floyd.

That morning I come into the stable yard about half past eight, and they had the mules all ready, and two wagons rigged out. A couple of stable niggers was throwing the dogs into the wagons. Over against the wall a man was leaning where the sun was, switching pebbles with a stick and talking to a big nigger boy with boots on. The nigger saw me coming and spoke to the man leaning on the wall. I said good morning when he looked up.

"Mornin," he said. He squinted out from under his hat.

"You Mister Pentland?"

"Nope. Name's Floyd."

"Mine's Les Webster. I come about the dogs."

"Well, I'm pleased to know you, Mister Webster. We's fixin to run the dawgs now. Want to get out while the coveys is still feedin in the open." He nodded toward the wagons, which were pulling off down the road. The nigger nodded toward the wagons, too, but when I looked at him, he looked down, grinning, to slap the dust off his boots. You could see he hadn't had them boots too long.

Floyd was rolling a cigarette with his free hand. "Time we get you rigged out with a woods pony, you can foller us down that road. Mister Pentland is meetin me an' the rigs over to Binny's Churchyard, an' we're workin out from there."

The nigger boy snickered at the way Floyd said "Mister" Pentland. Floyd looked at him a minute.

"This here's Buster," he said finally. "Buster'll get you a pony an' take you out to Binny's. I reckon Mister Pentland's the one to see if you take a likin to any of the dawgs."

Dewey Floyd switched a stone with his stick, then pushed himself away from the wall like he was tired and walked slowly across the yard. He was tall and skinny, dressed in a white field jacket and soiled khakis which hung out over his knee boots. There was something funny about the way he moved, just like the way he talked — sort of soft and quiet and not really getting any place, and that stick switching back and forth, slow, like the tail on a cat.

Buster come out of the stable now with two horses. I climbed on and headed after Floyd, and Buster right behind me, hollering at the other niggers to get out of his way.

Now he was prancing all over that red clay road, grinning like a damn fool. "Mistuh Dewey say ah's to take you out to Binny's Hant-yard."

"Yeah, I heard him."

"Yessuh."

Buster was making his horse prance by slapping the reins. He kept looking over at me to see if it was okay to talk. "Ah guess you-all ain' acquainted wid dese heah hants out to Binny's?"

"Who told you there was ghosts there, Buster?"

"Mistuh Dewey Floyd. Mistuh Dewey, he live a long time in de swamp. He say dey ain' no foolin' wid hants, an' ah don' truck wid 'em no time."

"Maybe he's ridin' you."

"Whuffo' he wan' go foolin' Bustuh? He ain' got no call to do dat."

Buster was staring at me, real uncertain. I didn't say nothing, only grinned.

"Now Mistuh Pentland, he say dey ain' none. He say Mistuh Dewey ain' no diff'rint den black folks. Don' seem like no hant gwine fool wid a Yankee man, ainyhow."

I looked at him then, and he turned away like he'd said something wrong. "He your boss?"

"Yessuh."

"How about Mister Floyd?"

"Yessuh. Bofe 'em. Leastways, de Yankee man's de boss o' de outfit, an' ah kinda wuks fo' him, but mos'ly ah wuks wid Mistuh Dewey Floyd. It's him dat got me de job. Ah's de spottah. When a dawg is p'intin', ah hollers, an' when a dawg is los', ah fines him."

Buster was grinning again, and slapping the reins on the horse's neck. He stretched his legs out in the stirrups so's both of us could get a look at his boots. We rode along and didn't talk no more.

I saw the dogs first, in the cornfield on the left past the Church-yard, running in among the broken stalks. There was a black-and-white setter paired off with a little lemon pointer. The two wagon rigs were lying back on the road, a nigger driving each, and two men on horses were watching from the edge of the field. One of them was Dewey Floyd. The other headed over to me and the nigger.

Buster stopped whistling. "Heah he come," he whispered. He swung his horse wide and galloped for the wagons, the man yelling at him all the way.

"Talk about your shiftless niggers! I'm surprised he got you out here, Mister Webster. My name's Joe Pentland."

Pentland turned his horse around and fell in beside me. "Both rigs are out, so you'll get a chance to see pretty well what we got. There's plenty of birds, so there's no trouble that way."

"You got a couple of nice-lookin' rigs there, Mister Pentland."

"Joe'll do fine. I guess first names are okay in the same business, huh?" Pentland laughed loudly, even for a big man. "What the hell," he said.

"Yeah," I said. He looked at me. "My name's Les," I said.

"Okay, Les. Yeah, the rigs are okay. Twelve dogs to a rig, two out at a time, and each rig's got a special dog for singles. The owner wants the best, and I guess I got it for him, all right. Les, you're gonna like these dogs. Just look at that Sadie bitch out there and tell me I ain't got a right to be proud."

Somebody had a right to be proud, for sure. The lemon pointer come out real pretty from behind a pile of stalks and swung into a tight point, and the setter right behind her.

"P'int!" hollers the nigger.

I watched Floyd.

"I guess you see how the setter dog's honorin' her point," said

11

Pentland. He laughed and spat on the ground.

Floyd was talking soft to the dogs: "Whoa-a-up, Sadie, eas-y, eas-y, whoo-a-up, Caesar, eas-y, boy, eas-y, eas-y . . . ."

Then the quail got up, and the way he handled the gun I knew he wouldn't miss: he took a bird off each side of the covey rise, neat as anything, and then he was talking again. "Daid, Caesar, daid, day-ud bird, Sadie, eas-y, eas-y . . . ."

"He's good with the dogs," I said. "Damn good."

"Hell, it's not him, it's the dogs." Pentland spat again, only a different way.

"Maybe, but they mind him good. And he's handy with that gun."

Pentland looked at me like I'd shot a dog by mistake. "He ain't been poachin' twenty years for nothin'! I ain't never seen the bastard miss a bird, but that don't mean nothin'. But for Joe Pentland, he'd be layin' up his time in the pokey. Wanted in three states for poachin', and when it ain't poachin', it's gettin' so cocky-eyed mean drunk that Jesus couldn't help him!"

Pentland was all red in the face and glaring at me. I didn't say nothing.

"Do *any* damn thing when he's like that! A man like him should stay in the woods with the rest of the animals, that's what I say. Meaner'n a snake."

I was surprised to see him getting so hot about a man, especially before a stranger. "I guess it ain't none of my affair," I said. "I just like the way he takes them dogs."

Floyd was walking slowly down the furrows to the horses, and the niggers let a new pair of dogs out of the rig.

"What in hell you let 'em do *that* for?" yelled Pentland, waving at the fresh dogs. "You know damned well I want to put Buddy and Tex onto the singles so's Mister Webster here can see 'em."

Pentland turned to me. "See what I mean, Les?"

I didn't answer him.

Dewey Floyd looked at Pentland kind of funny. Buster come up behind him. He spoke to Buster, still watching Pentland. "Buster, tell 'em to pull on around and put down Tex and Buddy."

That quiet way of speaking, like there was never anything wrong. He just walked over to his horse and slid the gun into the saddle holster, and Pentland rode out after the dogs and the nigger. The quail was mostly scattered along a ridge of loblolly pine over at the other side of the cornfield, and I headed after them.

Dewey Floyd rode up alongside. He yanked that stick of his out of the gun holster and took to swatting the dry stalks in half as he rode. His horse was used to that funny sound a stick makes, but mine's ears stuck up sharp, and he was all shivery under the saddle.

"Pentland's all riled about somethin', ain't he?" I said.

"Ain't he." Floyd repeated it softly. He took an extra hard cut at a cornstalk, and my horse jumped sideways. "Take keer on that pony," he said, not looking over. "He don't like no weight back o' the saddle, even yore hand."

"Might be the stick. What do you keep that around for?"

"Don't know for sure. Time I was livin in the woods, I kinda liked the feel of it in my hand."

I know he was looking me over, out from under his hat, and still switching the stick.

"I figger Pentland told you some about me?"

"Yeah. Yeah, he sorta did."

The way he was talking made me feel kind of funny.

"That's okay, Mister Webster, don't trouble yoreself none. He allers tells ever'body right off 'bout how he's the las' thing 'tween me and damnation." He laughed quietly, still looking at me the way a coon looks out of a tree. "He ain't told you nothin that ain't so, I guess. A feller'd never catch on that him and me's brother-in-laws. Maybe he ain't told you that part yet."

"Nope. What I mean is, you don't have to tell me nothin'."

"I reckon I don't, no. Don't pay me no mind, Mister Webster, I jes feels like talkin. Thing is, my sis has got herself married off to this here Pentland, an' that's how come I'm here. They don' want no poacher fer kin to the bes' dog trainer in Georgia, which folks say Pentland is, an' so they took me on long as I'd keep my nose clean. He's worryin hisself to death about that."

He laughed again. "Never knew a Yankee yet wasn't worryin on somethin," he added.

"It looks like you're doin' a good job," I said.

"Eatin's good. Job don't pay nothin to speak of, an' it ain't news that me and Pentland got no use fer the other. Hell, I'd go back to the woods but fer the dawgs. I'm gittin mighty attached to them dawgs. How'd that li'l Sadie 'pear to you?"

"She's good. You handled her good."

Floyd nodded his head. "She's a right fine dawg, Sadie is. I done all the work on her an' I'd like a lot to have her fer mine. These two ain't bad neither."

We were coming up behind Pentland. The sun was right back of the pines in front of us, so bright I could only just make out the dogs. They were close to twenty yards apart, both on nice points.

"Two sets of birds," said Floyd.

Pentland walked in fast, yelling at the setters to hold. He flushed two birds over the near dog, taking one, and swung over and killed a single that got up wild in front of the other dog after the first shot. He made it look harder than Floyd did, but a nice double all the same. Then he was yelling again, dead, dead, and they found the birds fast, only they brought 'em right over to Dewey Floyd.

"What do you want to go callin' 'em in like that for?" Pentland hollered at Floyd. "Dammit, you're goin' to fix these dogs so's they'll come to nobody else!"

He come stomping over toward us, and Buster behind him with his eyes bugging out.

"He didn't call 'em, Mister Pentland," I said, kind of uneasy.

"Seems like them ol' dawgs jes took a min' to come to Mistuh Dewey Floyd," whispered Buster, looking scared, and then Floyd had his horse over between Buster and Pentland.

"You Buster, get to hell back to them wagons," Floyd said. He cut Buster's horse across the rump with his stick, and the nigger lit out down the ridge and over the cornfield, all arms and legs and flapping leather.

That was it, right there. Talking soft and slow all the time, nice as hell to the dogs and niggers, and then he takes and cuts a horse like that.

Floyd didn't look at Pentland at all. He came back past me, grinning a funny grin, and saying, "Look at that nigger boy ride, Mister Webster, jes you look at that nigger boy ride."

Then he was trotting away, switching his stick in the dew grass, and the dogs right on his heels.

Pentland jammed his gun back in its saddle holster. He wasn't saying a thing. I turned my horse back, and pretty soon he caught up. He was glaring like I was supposed to say something.

"I'd like to get a look at some more of your dogs," I said.

The rest of the day there wasn't much trouble, and I got to see the whole of both rigs. I never seen two men handle dogs like Floyd and Joe Pentland; there wasn't much to be said between them except they run the dogs different ways. Maybe it come from being a poacher, but Floyd knew the country like he was a part of it, and right where the birds was every time. That takes a man that's lived in the woods alone.

I got back there a few weeks later with an order for the three best setters Pentland was selling and the lemon bitch pointer if I could get her.

You could see right away that things was different. Dewey Floyd was leaning against the stable like before, switching dust with the stick, and there was the nigger right beside him. I didn't know it was Buster right off because he didn't have no boots, and niggers generally look pretty much the same. But he said "Mawnin', Mistuh Webstuh," and I knew it was him, only he sure looked different without the boots.

Dewey Floyd peered out from under his hat.

"Mornin'," I said. "I come to take that pointer away from you."

"No you ain't." He said it like it didn't need no explanation.

Buster stared at Floyd, kind of fidgety. "Mistuh Webstuh, we-uns ain' wid de dawgs no mo'."

"Buster, you go on up to the house an' say that Mister Webster done come, you hear me?"

Buster shambled off, looking back over his shoulder. Floyd watched him go.

"Looks kinda sorry without them boots, now, don't he?"

"What happened?"

"Hell, I don't know . . . . One night las' week I lit into some rotgut, some o' thet sour mash, an' come back an' — well, there was a kind of a ruckus, an' now me'n Buster is workin here in the stable." Floyd was staring at the ground all the time, kind of tired and tight, watching the end of the stick fooling in the dust.

"I'm sorry to hear it. I sure liked the way you run them dogs."

Joe Pentland was coming down the road to the stable. Floyd was watching him all the time he was talking.

"You see, Mister Webster, a man like me ain't got no place with dawgs. A man what would do what I done, he's a sight better off in the woods. Some of these days I aim to go back, 'cause when I'm here, ain't nothin seems to go right."

Pentland said good morning. "I'm goin' right down to the pens and get them setters for you, Webster."

He went ahead, then stopped and looked at Floyd. "You ain't paid to lean on that wall, Floyd, but since you're so busy shootin' off your mouth, why not tell Mister Webster why I can't sell him the pointer bitch? Why don't you tell him that?"

Pentland turned to me. "You remember the dog I mean. Sadie. The dog *Mister* Floyd liked so well — liked so damned well that last week he come home here drunk and beat her to death with that stick there." He spat on the ground and walked off.

I didn't feel much like looking at Dewey Floyd right then, so I looked at the ground. All I could see was the stick switching back and forth, back and forth, in the dust in front of his shoes. It made me jumpier'n hell, and I glanced up at him.

Floyd was looking after Pentland in that funny way of his, not angry at all, just sort of funny. He went right on talking as if Pentland had never come by, but he didn't take his eyes off him a minute. "You see, I was mighty close to them dawgs, an' that li'l one were my fav'rit. Sadie were a real stylish dawg. I jes don't know rightly what it was, how I could come to doin it. But I did it, sure'n hell."

Dewey Floyd put his stick up under his arm and took out some paper and tobacco. He was talking so quietly I could hear the soft blowing and shifting of the horses through the wall behind him.

"Sober," he said, "I couldn't take this stick to no dawg that way, no more'n I could a pony nor a nigger. But a man . . ."

He paused a minute to fix the tobacco in his cigarette.

"Now you take a man . . . . Time comes, I reckon I could do that easier'n nothin." He ran his tongue along the sticking edge of the paper, squinting out at me from under his hat.

Atlantic Monthly
January 1951
An *Atlantic* "First"

The Fifth Day

Four days face to face with another man is a long time, especially four hot days of waiting in a Coast Guard dinghy on Peconic Bay. The morning of the fifth day, Dave Winton stiffened once more as he eased the dragging hook over the side for the last time, winced a moment later at the "thunk" of the twin hook tossed heavily into the water on the other side of the boat and the vicious hum of the outgoing line sawing back and forth over the gunwales. Joe put his out that way because it was handier, but to Dave the method made an uneasy difference: Joe's hook, if only because of the haste with which it plunged each morning into the bay, was the one which was sure to find the body.

Dave secured his line around the middle seat and turned to Joe for instructions. Joe Robitelli was already settled comfortably in the stern, just as he'd been for four days: he hadn't even changed his shirt. The oars were untouched on the floor of the dinghy.

"You want me to start, Joe?"

"Start? Start what?"

"The oars. We have to keep dragging, don't we?"

"The picket boat's gone, ain't it?" Joe shrugged his shoulders and lay back.

"Sure, but you said the body always shows up on the fifth day."

"That's right. Today or tomorrow, or for sure the day after."

Dave stared at him. Joe dragged a small canvas bag from beneath his head. "Look," he said, "Good Old Joe finally got wise

17

to himself."

He hauled two hand lines and a wet bait package out of the bag and spread them triumphantly on the stern seats. "How about that, Dave? And I got six cans of beer to go with it. A regular fishing party."

"You said we were sure to find the guy today."

Joe stared back at him. Their faces were uncomfortably close in the drifting boat, and Dave watched him speaking: "Look, for Christ's sake, I been tellin you to relax for four days now, and today I get you all fixed up here with fish lines and beer, and you're still yappin!"

With their faces so close together, the voice seemed to come from somewhere behind him.

"Okay," Dave said, "that was fine the first four days, but sooner or later, we're supposed to find this guy. Maybe we're right on top of him now."

"Look, we ain't supposed to do nothing but sit out here, so we might as well have a good time for ourselves. If the guy comes up, the guy comes up, but while we're waitin for him, I robbed some bacon from the galley for bait and got us six beers as a present from the lighthouse boys."

Dave glanced restlessly at Joe's present, then watched him rig some bacon rind onto the hooks. Joe, glancing at him, winked and sang mournfully, "We three — are all a-lone —" with pointed emphasis on the "three," and winked again. Dave bent over for the oars to hide the irritation in his expression; they were pressed against the side of the boat by Joe's ankle. "What's up, Joe?"

"What's up, Dave?" Joe studied the baited hooks, his brows wrinkled in concentration.

"Look, I'll do the rowing if you don't want to."

"Take it easy, kid. Relax. Have a Pabst Blue Ribbon Beer."

"What about those people waiting on shore? What do you want to do, Joe, keep them waiting all week?"

"Take it easy, will ya? They're gonna wait anyway. Just take it easy." There was a taint of irritation in Joe's voice which spoiled his smile.

Dave stared at the water eddying silently around the dragging line. Those gloomy people on the pier in their new vacation clothes, and this guy bragging about beer and bacon. To hell with him. Right now the hooks were fumbling along the belly of the bay like two clubfeet, scraping and turning and raking the seaweed off the rocks in search of the drowned man. This very moment they could be pulling through the rotten clothes like fingernails through soggy paper.

Dave grimaced and looked at Joe. The latter was leaning back, arms spread and a fish line in each hand, his white cap over his eyes and a cigarette loose in his mouth.

"I guess I'll row awhile, just for the hell of it, Joe."

Joe shrugged his shoulders and took his foot away from the oars. His silence irritated Dave. He said: —

"You don't have to worry about my getting you in trouble," realizing the idea was ridiculous even before Joe hitched one of the fish lines around a cleat and pushed the cap back with the free hand, unveiling a stare of disbelief.

"What in hell do you mean by that, Davey Boy?"

"Nothing." Dave licked his lips. "I just don't feel right about those people ashore, I guess."

"I don't give a good goddam *how* you feel about them people ashore. Didn't the Old Man tell em go home and wait, but no, they gotta camp out here and raise a stink till we find him. They'd be yellin at us to get out here if there was a hurricane goin on, especially the ones like you, with a lot of dough and no sense. All we're out here for is to make em happy thinkin we're doing somethin, understand? We ain't even got a outboard motor."

Joe sucked violently on his cigarette.

"So don't give me this crap about gettin me in trouble, Sonny Boy. The Old Man himself wouldn't act no different than what I'm doin. I been at this game a long time, and you ain't nothin but a kid, I don't care how much dough you got, just remember that."

There was nothing to offer in defense of a wealthy family: Dave pulled the oars quietly. Joe was still glaring at him as the tension evaporated between their faces.

Then Joe laughed shortly, pulling his cap back over his eyes. "Look, Dave, all I'm sayin is, this bay's six miles across, and all we got is two lousy draggin hooks and a ten-foot dinghy. There ain't a prayer of findin the guy."

"Okay. Maybe I feel like getting a little exercise."

Joe flicked his cigarette over the side. It stuck on the flat bay water like a leaf on the mud. "Yeah," he said. "That's what you wanna do, Davey, get a little exercise."

Dave cut viciously at the bland-faced water, and the oar, skating over the surface, arched a leaf of spray onto Joe's shirt. Joe's thick brown hand came up slowly, pushed its fingers over the drops, then drifted upwards to his cap, which was pushed back over the forehead. His eyes opened slightly, bright with a momentary suspicion, but widened abruptly at the spectacle of Dave's reddening face. One hazel eye winked in a sleepily patronizing manner before the thick hand rose again, methodic as a derrick, adjusted the cap over the eyes, and fell back over the stern.

Any day but today he might have been a stumpy Italian fisherman sleeping in the sun, his short legs sprawled in the bottom of any small boat in the world, but today he was a tough Brooklyn guinea with his cap over his eyes and a smelly shirt on his back, who didn't give a damn for the water, the sun, the morning, but especially not for the drowned man softening somewhere beneath them, nor the frightened family in their new vacation clothes who waited for the fifth day on the pier.

Dave spat noisily into the water. It was bad enough rowing around in the sun with two hooks dragging without having to watch a guy like this take it easy three feet away. And worst of all, Joe was right. There was no sense in rowing, no sense at all.

Dave rowed furiously, then rested the oars again. He watched the water fall in pointless drops from the blades. The body was sure to be off in the other direction.

Amusement deepened on Joe's face; Dave waited for the brown hand to rise to the cap, then dipped the oars again in the teeth of the smile. But the smile judged him with confidence: —

"How you doin, Dave?"

"All right. It's getting kind of hot."

"Yeah, it must be. That's okay, though, long as you're gettin your exercise, ain't that right, Dave?"

The smile broadened. Joe pulled a pack of cigarettes out of his breast pocket and flicked one up. Dave refused it with a nod.

"The fish ain't bitin so good." Joe pulled the cigarette from the pack with his lips. "I guess there was plenty to eat the last few days here in the bay."

Joe secured the fish lines to the stern cleats and brought his hands up behind his head, chuckling at the subtlety of the implication.

"Why not boat them oars and take it easy, Davey Boy. You ain't provin nothin."

"I'm not trying to."

"Okay." He was watching Dave pull the oars in over his lap, and Dave, uneasy, drew a cigarette from his own pocket and lit it before he remembered. He glanced at Joe's expression.

"First of all you didn't like the fish lines and beer, and now my cigarettes ain't good enough for you," it said.

"I didn't feel like one a minute ago," Dave said. Joe didn't answer. They sat still in the hot boat until he spoke.

"I guess you got a lot of dough in your family, huh, Dave?"

"Lay off, Joe. What difference does it make?"

"No difference. I'm just askin. It ain't nothin to be ashamed of." Joe opened a can of beer without looking at it. "Like this guy we're lookin for, he wasn't ashamed of it. He bought himself a little boat to take the family joy-ridin."

"So what?"

"So he got himself drowned." Joe laughed.

"And you're not sorry for those people?"

"Sure I'm sorry. Sorry as hell. Still and all, they shoulda gone home like they was told."

"So we're not going to do a thing."

"Sure. We're gonna float around and look at the scenery until the guy pops up and asks for a beer."

Joe was smiling again, but the corners of his smile pointed down instead of up. Dave shifted on the seat. The sun was hot on his back, and his legs were cramped. What in hell was so funny. From where he sat, Joe's grin looked six inches across. And dumbly, he watched Joe lean forward and lift the oars from the oarlocks and lay them along the gunwales on top of the seats: total defeat, and to resist would be to expose himself again.

He eased himself onto the floor of the forward part of the dinghy, his back to Joe.

"That's a-boy, Dave, relax. Enjoy the scenery."

Joe's laugh ruffled through his hair, fell back with a triumphant clatter into the stern. Good Old Joe. One more smile and he'd ram an oar down Good Old Joe's throat: suppose that family was watching them from shore? Even the drowned man must be waiting for them now. He might be two inches under the dinghy, or rubbing softly against the drifting hull. Perhaps even Joe was nervous about him. People said he'd pop up like a rubber ball on the fifth day.

Dave stirred uncomfortably as he peered at the water of the bay. Not a sound, not even a gull. Just the heat and the dry paint smell of the dinghy and Good Old Joe in the stern, worrying about someone else's wife. Dave laughed at this idea, and the laugh caused a suspicious stir behind him.

Joe's voice was loud in the silence of the bay. "You hear how it happened?" The tone was innocent.

"How what happened?"

"The rich guy." Joe pronounced the words slowly. "The rich guy that got himself drowned."

"Oh yeah, the rich guy. The rich guy that got himself drowned." Dave paused. "Well, the way I heard it, Joe, this rich guy bought himself a little boat to take his family joy-riding and got himself drowned."

Under the noon sun, Dave's rage swarmed through him like fruit flies in a heated jar. He crouched in wait for Joe's reaction, afraid at the same time to turn and face it. Joe's tone, however, conveyed no hint of the wound.

"That's right, Dave, but how did it happen?"

"I don't know exactly," he parried. "The guys told me he tried to make it ashore to get help after they capsized."

"He tried to make it ashore okay, so he could save his own tail. I guess you thought he was a goddam hero or somethin."

"Yeah, I guess I did. I guess I thought he was a goddam hero or something."

"Well he ain't. He run out on his wife and kids." Joe's voice was suddenly angry. "It's bad enough havin these rich guys get salty on us and gettin hung up on sand bars and makin us risk our necks to save theirs, but I never thought they was all yella."

The words of exchange hung in the silence overhead as if unwilling to drift away over the empty bay.

"Oh sure." Dave nodded his head philosophically. "That's the thing about rich guys, Joe. You wouldn't believe it, Joe, but all rich guys are yellow. The richer the guy, the wider the yellow streak, every time."

Dave turned to face Joe, excited to see his smile waver, fall away entirely.

"Don't get smart with me, Davey Boy. I'm wise to you. Just don't try that sarcastic line on me, understand?"

"What's the trouble, Joe?"

"Look, Sonny, I'm warnin you, don't get so smart if you don't want a smack in the mouth 'll last you a long time, understand. So watch yourself."

Dave eyed Joe a moment in silence, vaguely conscious of the beer smell on his breath. He felt his own smile flutter mournfully on his face, like a white flag in a dead man's hand; it didn't belong there, not because he was afraid but because the game was over, and now he was suddenly so angry that he spoke with difficulty, in a gasping, distant voice: "C'mon, Joey Boy, relax. Smile. Laugh.

You don't care about the rich guy, you're just out here for the laughs, remember?"

Joe didn't hit him, only flipped his beer can over the side and hauled in the fish lines. And aware for the first time of the picket boat coming up behind, Dave groped aimlessly for the bow line. Joe grinned as they rigged the lowered pulley to the dinghy. "It's okay to shoot your mouth off with the boat comin, Davey Boy, but I'm gonna take you up behind the boathouse soon as we tie up."

He watched Joe's raucous reception on the boat, his easy way with the other men, and going back, Dave's anger fizzled away in wide, erratic circles over the bay, like a stray wasp, until it disappeared entirely. The boat was early, he'd made a fool of himself, and he was going to have his head knocked off for nothing. They hadn't even found the drowned man. To hell with the drowned man, anyway.

Dave stepped onto the pier and turned to wait for Joe. Joe stood foremost in a grinning knot of men; Dave sensed that he was expected to act, and turned away. He stopped short at the sight of the corpse.

The water was sliding out of the drowned man's clothes and escaping through the slats of the pier. Dave listened to its uneven tick on the dead water around the pilings. The terrible apathy of the carcass only made him wonder why they hadn't wrapped it up in canvas and taken it away before the family arrived. Joe was right: they should have gone. This thing couldn't mean anything to them any more.

Looking away, he saw the Old Man coming down the road to the pier, attended by two men with a stretcher, but the breeze, tacking momentarily, shocked him back into the dead man's presence. He stepped away, shouldering Joe.

"That's why they come for us early," Joe said. "The fifth day, just like I told you."

Joe glanced at the bulging mask and turned back to Dave.

"Five days in the water don't do much for a guy." He studied Dave's expression.

"He don't look much like a hero, huh, Dave? Imagine a family hangin around five days to have a look at that."

Dave stared at the face again and sat down abruptly on the edge of the pier. "Leave him alone," he muttered, his voice far away.

"I ain't botherin him one little bit."

When Joe laughed, Dave opened his eyes. He saw the proferred cigarette in the dark hand, but he could not move. Joe tapped the cigarette against the back of the hand.

"Here they come," he said.

They watched the drowned man's family approach the foot of the pier, like a knot of sheep unsure of their footing, then glanced at the stretchermen, who were pushing the body onto a rusty square of canvas.

"Snap it up, you guys, give 'em a break." Joe's tone was urgent under his breath. "C'mon, Dave," he said. He headed down the pier with the picket boat crew.

Dave stood up, but his legs moved uncertainly. The sun was very hot. He watched the other men meet and pass the oncoming family, both groups moving shyly, in single file. Following Joe Robitelli's example, most of the men had removed their caps.

Atlantic Monthly
September 1951

Midnight Turning Gray

Once, when approaching the hospital by the side road through the woods, she knew she would round the final bend to find it gone — not gone, precisely, but sunk back into that coarse New England hillside like a great crushed anthill, its denizens so many mad black dots darting in and out and over the dead earth. Earlier she had imagined that the season here was always autumn, and she struggled still with an idea that the inmates, in some essential way, did not exist at all.

But Lime Rock State Mental Hospital surged out from behind the corner of the wood, awaiting her. Her heart quickened: if the sun shines here, she thought irrationally, it must shine everywhere.

She was relieved to see the buildings. There were always figures on the woods road, figures whose status or intent was never certain. And patients, as one of the nurses had once warned her, tried now and then to get away. In her caution, Anne Pryor perceived in all strange faces on the grounds a certain secretive sly sickness, and was glad each morning of the protection of the buildings, where the ill were organized like livestock and dealt with by authority.

The buildings, eleven in all, maintained a firm identity, though their shapes and functions were quite separate. The wings of each extended towards the recesses of others, in a pattern like a puzzle pulled apart, and unless one knew one's way — as Anne, though three weeks here, was certain she did not — the puzzle seemed malevolent and confusing. The roofs of these buildings were slate and steep, overhanging dark grilled porches set into the ends, like caves, and the windows, hollow-eyed and barred, crouched back in brick of a rufous earthen color. This color pervaded the place, even to the lifeless ground on which it stood.

For though Lime Rock Hospital had stood for thirty years, it had never been absorbed by the countryside. Rather than creep forward to camouflage its outline, the growth on this New England hill had seemed to shrink away, leaving it more and more exposed. The grass was thin, and the earth maintained its excavated look. It had a violent iron smell, like blood.

This morning the smell was muted by the new November cold. Leaving the car in the yard behind the Administration Building, Anne took a last deep breath before entering its basement by the fire door. In the converted boiler room Dr. Sobel and Mrs. McKittredge and Harry Marvin were having coffee. Dr. Sobel put down his cup as Anne entered the room and said good morning to her as he left. Every day Dr. Sobel, an odd soft little man with a Phi Beta Kappa key, moved a little more quickly, more intensely, towards the wards. He called them "the Augean Stables." The term was facetious, and Dr. Sobel was not a facetious man. He used it only because he did not want people to tell him — as Mrs. McKittredge, or "Mac" as she was called, had long since told him — that, for his own sake, he ought to recognize the element of hopelessness in his task.

"He's going to die here, is old Doc Sobel, and he may be a patient by the time he does." Harry Marvin, twenty-eight, was sallow and dark, with a long cropped head and a manner which was not Harvard, as he imagined, but only rather effeminate. He had been, in the war, a Pharmacist's Mate, and on this slim medical background based his opinion, shared by Anne, six years his junior, that she had neither the experience nor the temperament to work here.

"Mental hospitals, " Mac remarked, "must settle for what they can get." In saying this, she implied no criticism of Dr. Sobel but was simply stating for the first time that day her favorite fact. Mac was a social worker, and unlike Sobel, was less concerned with the patients than with their treatment at the hands of the state. "And what do they get?" she demanded. "They get the Sobels, who are too starry-eyed to see that two thirds of what their salaries should be go for the mushrooms on those fat crooks' steaks. They get the Harry Marvins, whose medical training couldn't qualify them for a job in an Old Dog's Home. And they fill in with little student nurses and nice kids like Anne, who are overworked for nothing!"

"Well, they have *you* anyway, Mac," Anne said, her tentative laugh defeating the remark.

"That's true," Mac said, and grinned obligingly. Between her fingers a permanent cigarette, goaded by a mannish thumb, flicked up and down like the tail of a nervous bird.

"I've got to get over to the Monkey House," Harry Marvin said. Harry worked in the Children's Wards, and like Dr. Sobel, had given his task a name. Anne had once thought that the term referred to the usual clamor of children, or that it bore, perhaps, a "cute-as-monkeys" context. But on her first visit there, her senses explained it far more harshly. And its aptness breached a strict staff code by which all inmates were thought of, and referred to, as "patients," though the majority were beyond all aid and went untreated, even by Dr. Sobel.

Mac's wry wrinkled face winced openly at the remark, but she said nothing. She was a practical woman, and clearly she knew that Harry Marvin did his work, and, however flippant, did it very well. Nevertheless Mac disapproved. She seemed to sense a danger that Anne, too, had recognized already, that if, even for one moment, they were to acknowledge the degradation of their charges, to regard them openly as unworthy of respect and love, to regard them as sub-human — if once, in short, they succumbed to uneasy laughter, then all pretense would disappear, and the hospital would no longer be a hospital but a prison.

Harry Marvin knew this, too. Glancing at them, he frowned, discomfited. "Well, I'm off," he said, after a moment. "You, too, Anne?"

"She hasn't had her coffee," Mac rebuked him.

"No, I don't need it, Mac." Anne's tone of breathless apology, abetted by a startled, mournful look, was characteristic of her manner. Inviting protection, it drew people to her, yet she felt at times that she spoke too loudly, even bumptiously, and was conscious of a certain coarseness in her stance and gait more becoming, her mother had told her pointedly, to a tall boy of thirteen. Though pretty in an impermanent way, she had not yet learned to show herself to best advantage.

Or so said Harry Marvin, the very first time she had spoken with him alone. Lonely, she had sought him out because he was her generation and might supply the friendship essential to her here. But Harry had no time for frivolity. His was the clinical approach, and during their second talk, he made a number of observations on her sexual patterns, or rather, the absence of them: disguised in his white frock, his fingertips together, he had lured her into admission of inexperience. As a cure he prescribed his own caress, and when she refused it without quite meaning to, accused her of being neurotic. His astonishment suggested that any girl resisting him might well end her days as a patient in Lime Rock State Mental Hospital. He went on to discuss her appetites, sublimated, he assured her, because as an only child she needed to dominate her widowed mother. Anne sought for the missing link in his diagnosis, which seemed a rash *non sequitur* and was, besides, inaccurate. Her mother, poor but proud, clung to her good family name and had never been dominated by anybody. But Anne, embarrassed by his use of the word "appetites," nodded meekly in agreement. Too insecure to spy insecurity in another, she was anxious only to change the subject.

Anne and Harry walked in silence up the stairs and out the front door and along the driveway towards Anne's building. The driveway continued down the slope to the front gate, which hid in the maple trees off the highway. So as to draw less attention to the hospital and its unwelcome presence in the township, the staff and the rare visitors were encouraged to use the back road through the woods. The precaution seemed foolish since the mass of raw structures, like a glacial deposit on its hillside, was a landmark for miles around. Yet its approaches were obscure, there were few signs, though bald and exposed on its terrain of broken, rocky fields, the hospital, as one came nearer, sank out of sight into the woods.

"I suppose Mac took offense at my reference to the Monkey House." They had paused at the door of Anne's Occupational Therapy Unit, which formed part of the ground floor of one of the buildings.

"Oh, I don't think so. She knows you were only joking."

"Listen, if you don't want to get like Sobel, you have to relax once in a while, that's all. And the Monkey House is the most depressing ward in the place. I mean, you always *hope* in there, and you're always disappointed. So many of those kids are basically sound, or would be if only —"

"I know!" Anne said. "Have you met Ernest Hamlin?"

Harry, interrupted, shook his head in irritation. "Who's Ernest?" he said.

"Oh, he's a patient. He comes to O.T. now. But I mean, he's basically sound. I've *talked* to him," Anne offered as proof, speaking faster and faster. "He says —"

"Maybe they all are," Harry said, and turned his back on her.

"Ernest Hamlin really is, though," Anne said. She watched him go, then turned and entered the outside door, unhappy. The inner door required a key, and she paused to hunt for it in her purse. As usual, she was very nervous, and today, upset by Harry

Marvin, she dropped the key upon the floor.

On her first visit to the Occupational Therapy Unit — and surely this unit was the mildest in all of Lime Rock, since only patients in control of themselves were allowed here without special supervision — she had felt a revulsion based on fear which passed immediately to vertigo and nausea. She had had to sit down, perspiring and cold. It had frightened her, that revulsion, since it was so baseless. There was nothing fearsome about the patients at O.T. Perhaps if they hadn't gazed at her in that wide-eyed way, perhaps if the ward hadn't smelled of children, of crude clay bowls, and varnish, paint, of balsa wood and cardboard games, of apples and faint urine in the makeshift clothes . . .

Thus she was grateful for Ernest Hamlin.

Earnest had come the previous Tuesday, at the hour of the weekly square dance. The square dance, for Anne, was the most upsetting occasion of her week. It elicited a forlorn gaiety in the patients, and it was grotesque in its laughter without merriment, in the heavy aimless prancing, in the pairing off of illness and of age. Here a wan old woman clutched a dreaming black man; there a smiling student nurse propped up a bashful moron. Beyond, a lank-haired catatonic in a knee-length Twenties frock performed wild stumbling pirouettes all by herself. Along the walls the others watched, despairing, giggling, or excited by the din, some clapping vaguely out of time with the piano.

"Don't you want to dance?" Anne cried.

"No, thank you, Miss," said a big fair boyish man poised for escape by the door to the room where some played shuffleboard, and for a moment Anne imagined him a visitor.

"I haven't seen you here before," she ventured. He faced her then and smiled.

"Oh, I'm a patient all right, Miss," he said.

"I see," she said, and, ineffectual, flushed. "My name is Anne."

"Mine's Ernest Hamlin." He enclosed her outstretched hand in his. "I come down to do something with my hands" — he held them out and gazed at them — "so's I wouldn't go nuts." He smiled again at her involuntary start, then sat down carefully on the edge of a folding chair.

She seated herself beside him.

"I ain't really nuts, you see, Miss, not yet, anyways." He glanced pointedly at the dancers. "I guess these poor dopes claim that quite a lot."

"Nobody here is really 'nuts,' Mr. Hamlin," she blurted dutifully. "They only —"

"You know what I mean, Miss," Ernest told her. "Men-tally

ill. I ain't really mentally ill, not yet, anyways." Again he observed the dancers, wincing. "I'll make the grade, though, one of these fine days."

"You mustn't feel sorry for yourself," Anne said. "You mustn't —"

"No?" he said. His heavy face turned to her once again. It was an intelligent face, rueful, perceptive, alight with quiet humor, quite different from the gallery of faces in the room. He was not yet dead in the way that people died here, their hair first, then the mouth and eyes, all but the hands. At Lime Rock hands, like infants' hands, or those of the old man frozen in his chair beside them, clung to life, whether clenched or groping. "No, maybe I shouldn't," Ernest said, and frowning, changed the subject.

"Do most of these folks know why they're here?" he said.

"The ones aware of anything do. They don't believe it, most of them." She waited for him.

"Oh, I *believe* it, all right," he told her quickly. "There ain't no doubt about what *I* got. I got a piece of shrapnel sitting too close in to my brain to operate, see? They can't operate. And every once in a while this shrapnel sort of acts up, like, and drives me nuts with pain — mentally ill with pain," he corrected himself. "I get so's I don't know what I'm doing even, see, I get destructive. I'm supposed to be dangerous, Miss, because I don't know what's going on. So this Vet's hospital, they give up on that piece of shrapnel after a while, they classify me a mental case, they got no provisions for guys like me, and they send me here. I didn't even get no chance to go on home and see my folks, or the boys in my shop, or nothing. And I got a mother waiting home, and sisters, and I got a part interest in this machine shop home. I'm a machinist." He gazed at his hands again, big useful hands sitting idle on his knees. "A damned good one, too," he muttered angrily. "I worked for them there at the hospital sometimes, and the guy running the shop, the super there, he said he never seen better work, and that's a fact." He shook his head. "Which is why I come down here this afternoon, I thought maybe you had some tools and stuff, a lathe, maybe, but there ain't nothing here but shuffleboard, and knitting needles, and games for kids."

She nodded, mute.

"So that's about it: they sent me up here, and I ain't mentally ill. My fiancee wrote me a letter already. She said it would be better to make a clean break. She said it hurt her worse'n it did me." Ernest Hamlin almost smiled. "But I'm just a young guy, I got a long life ahead of me, and guess where it looks like I'm going

to spend it —" He stopped short, as if shocked anew by the realiza-
tion. "Jesus," he whispered, "I can't believe it."

He set back gently upon her feet a fat, loose-lipped girl in
baggy dungarees who had square-danced into him and fallen. The
girl put her hands on her hips and swaggered with gross coyness
away from him. Her dancing partner was a scraggy female who
carried her head shot forward like a turkey and seemed on the
point of tears.

"So I feel sorry for myself," he concluded.

Anne nodded, overcome.

He cocked his head, alert to her emotion. "I didn't want to
trouble you, Miss. You were just being nice listening to all that
stuff, doing your job. A lot of the staff around here are pretty
tough," he added.

"They have to be tough," Anne said. "That doesn't mean that
they're not nice."

"Yeah, I guess that's right. Like this guy they got in charge of
the Disturbed Ward. This guy is out of this world. I mean, they
put *me* in there at first, with all them foul balls. Maybe you ain't
never seen that ward. They got about fifteen nuts in there, the
dangerous ones, except they ain't dangerous all the time, most of
them. He's got some beauties in there, this guy. The first day he
takes me by the arm, like a priest or something, and he says,
'C'mon, Ernest, I want you to meet the boys.' The boys are sitting around a table shelling peas, all but one. 'That's Phil,' the
guy says. 'Phil's a nice fellow, but he bites. You let Phil get his
teeth into you, and you're in trouble. He has to be pried off. So
You'd better keep a little distance when you talk to Phil.' This
Phil is sitting in the corner making a lot of racket, moaning and
grunting and all. I didn't feel much like talking to him, then or
later, although I *did* give it a whirl one day. Some conversation!
I don't think he *could* talk, if you want to know the truth, he was
in pretty bad shape. I mean, he *looked* bad, like some loony in the
movies or something, like the way I thought they *all* looked here
before I come here. Anyway, this superintendent, or whatever you
call him, *he* chats with Phil all the time. You'd think they was
buddies from way back. And he talks to them other birds the same
way. The others don't look as bad as Phil, they can mostly talk
and all. They gave me the creeps, though. When I was introduced,
I said, 'Hi, Boys.' Not a peep out of them, not one of them. They
all just watch me, sitting at the table with them peas. The super
acts like everything is hunky-dory. 'Pull up a chair,' he says to
me, 'and get acquainted.' Then one of these guys picks up a pea
and rolls it across the table at me. I catch it as it goes over the

edge. 'Thanks a lot, Bill,' I says — I'd caught his name, see — and I eat the goddam pea. This Bill flashes me a kind of smile. Then another guy starts hollering that I'm eating up all his peas, he wants to know why he's shelling in the first place, he pays his taxes, don't he, he ain't no lousy kitchen help. So this Bill gives me a big wink and knocks the other guy's bowl of peas into his lap and all over the floor. Just like that. And winks again. He *likes* me, see. And this other guy — I expected all hell to break loose, but it didn't — this other guy, he gets down on his knees and picks up all his peas one by one, and when he comes up for air he's grinning. Not really grinning, but watching this Bill in kind of a crafty way, like, and humming and nodding his head, and you could tell he was going to fix Bill for keeps, later on, he had it all figured out, only he never did. And then — listen, do you want to hear about all this, or do you want me to shut up?"

"No, please go on, Mr. Hamlin. I've never been in that ward, it's interesting."

"Yeah, it is," Ernest nodded in agreement. "But I appreciate you listening. I ain't had much chance to talk to nobody I could talk to. I talked some to the super in that ward, though. What a guy. He talked to me like I was the only one in there who could understand. That's the way he talked to all of them, even Phil — as if they were the only normal ones in the outfit. I don't know what he said to the others about me. He probably said, "Watch out for that goddam Ernest, boys, he's mentally ill, he'll break your back as quick as look at you!""

Ernest burst out laughing, and the sound rose high and loud against the clamor of feet and music and broken voices. Anne stared at him, dismayed. He was laughing so violently that in the animal closeness of the room, he had to loosen his collar. But now he coughed and stopped, as quickly as he had started. "No," he murmured, "I ain't the kind to hurt nobody if I can help it. Even in Korea, I didn't like it." He sat there for a moment in silence, then got to his feet. "Goodbye," he said, and went through the door of the shuffleboard room before she could think to call him back.

When he appeared the following afternoon, Anne felt unaccountably relieved. He wore a tie this time, of a deep green cheap material which bulged and twisted the collar of his denim shirt. Though the tie flew in her honor, he did not approach until he saw she was unoccupied. Then he came immediately and said, "I been thinking about what you told me about how I oughtn't to feel sorry for myself —"

And she wanted to say, Oh, I didn't mean it, I was talking

foolishly, you have every right . . .

" — and that's true, what you said, but I still do." He was clearly ashamed but continued doggedly, as if making a compulsory address. "Why I feel sorry is, I'm so damned useless. I can't *do* nothing, even for somebody else. I just got to sit here until I rot!"

"No, listen, Mr. Hamlin —"

"Jesus, call me Ernie, will you, Anne!" he cried, throwing his big hands into the air in a gesture of pain. Sheepish, he followed her to a seat at the side of the room.

"Listen, Ernie, maybe you can help us here. The staff needs help, it's much too small. Look, I'm in O.T. with one nurse today, and two wards coming in. We can't handle everybody properly. If you could —"

"Sure, sure, I know. I already talked to that super in the Disturbed Ward, before he got me transferred. I asked him if there wasn't something around for me to do, and he said, no, they couldn't pay me nothing, there wasn't enough salary to go around as it was. Can you beat that? For a job like that, locked up twelve months a year with those foul balls? Knowing they might jump him every time he turns his back? And that ain't why he's nice to them, either, he's just nice, that guy, and he's got guts!" Ernie, excited in his admiration, had forgotten momentarily about himself. "If I ever get out of here, I'm going to talk to somebody about that pay he gets! He ain't complaining, but he says himself he wouldn't do it only he's scared what kind of a creep would replace him for that kind of money. So he keeps on doing it, year after year after lousy year!"

Anne nodded, watching him. He was pounding his fist into his palm, beside himself. After a moment, she murmured, "Ernie, I wasn't thinking about a salaried job. I just thought you might be interested in helping out when you felt like it. It would keep you busy, and be a real contribution."

"Oh, sure. I mean, I'd be glad to help, Anne. I was thinking about a *job*, though, maybe outside, mowing lawns or something. That way, if I got a little money I could send it on home. That way, I could kid myself that I was helping to support my mother or something, you see?" He turned to her, his face pale. "Because another thing I figured out last night was that the best thing that could happen to me if I'm going to have to stay in this place —" and his tone suggested that he had yet to face this fact — "is that I go nuts. I mean, really honest-to-God mentally ill. Then maybe I won't care no more, and get a big bang out of square dancing with all my buddies."

"Ernie, please listen."

He shook his head, masochistic now, determined to have it out with himself. "It wouldn't be so hard," he muttered. "If people ain't nuts when they come in to this place, they sure as hell must be by the time they get out. You can't keep company like this and not have some of it rub off." He nodded bitterly at an old woman across the room who was remarking at the top of her voice upon the fact that staff members had no right to occupy themselves with just one patient, when other patients such as herself needed their pillows straightened behind their heads. "See that," he said. "She knows I like to talk to you, need to talk to you just to keep from going under, and she's going to do her best to pull me down there with the rest of them. Well, she'll make it yet."

"This isn't like you," Anne said, thinking to shame him. She knew her concern was partly selfish, since his self-control, and the companionship it guaranteed, were essential to her as well.

"No, it isn't," Ernie admitted. He glanced at her, as if to inquire how she knew. "I guess it's because you're kind of a doctor, like." He frowned. "You ain't, though, right? You're just a kid trying to help these people. Well, you're helping me, whether you know it or not." He blushed and stood up. "Forget, it, okay, Anne? I ain't going to bother you no more."

"You haven't bothered me," Anne told him truthfully. "I like to talk to you."

"Sure, sure." He had his back to her, hands in pockets. "So what do you want me to do to help you out?" he said, after a moment. "Shall I break that old woman's neck?"

They laughed together, disheartened.

"Just talk to people, Ernie. Help me talk to people. I run out of words after a while."

"I ought to be good at that. I never run out of words in my life, as I guess you found out." He grimaced, dismissing her protest with a gesture of his hand. "Okay. What'll I talk to them about?"

"Ernie," she said.

He paused, then turned to her, waiting.

"Look, you mustn't feel badly about telling me everything," she started. "If I were in your shoes, they'd have to drag me around screaming."

Still he waited.

"Only I guess you'll have to make the best of it. I hope you'll talk to me whenever you want." As always when she was ill at ease, she talked faster and faster. "And I admire your courage, and I'm going to try to help you."

"Help me?"

"Yes. I don't think you belong in here. I think it's unfair," Anne said, and regretted the impulse, afraid. "There probably isn't much I can do." She backed down before his breathless gaze, which hardened, then softened again. He was gentle enough to pretend she had not raised his hopes. He said,

"There's nothing you can do about it, Anne, thanks, anyway." He turned away again. "See you later," he said. Across the room, the old woman observed his approach with suspicion. She drew her heels up on the rung of her chair and clutched at her skirt, as if there was water on the floor.

Anne went to Harry Marvin for advice.

"You've been too protected," he said, answering her question, "you have no real knowledge of life, I mean. Why did you volunteer to work at Lime Rock? Why are you suddenly so concerned about Hamlin? Because you are interested medically in the patients? Or sociologically, even? Because you really want to help them? No. You came because your college education in the fine arts is worthless in any job which wouldn't bore you, and because you don't need a salary, and because a young girl ought to 'do something' while waiting to get married. People like you contribute nothing to society and therefore have an inner need for a cause. That's why you want to help him, Anne. You need a cause."

Satisfied with his diagnosis, he had walked away, as if nothing further need be said, as if her inquiry about Ernest Hamlin had not been of the slightest consequence. She wanted to run after him and boot him in the behind, having perceived that he resented the subject of Ernest Hamlin after her interruption of his speech this morning, and was sulking. Yet she was much less angry than hurt, for perhaps, in his cruelty, he had been right. But was it so wrong, she thought, to want a cause? Or had he meant that her cause was selfish, false?

Unlike Mac and Sobel and the others, yes, and even Harry Marvin, she could not quite accept the patients as sick human beings. Before her talks with Ernest Hamlin, they had been unreal to her, and her pity — which, until Harry intruded, she imagined had led her to volunteer — had remained intellectual. She had constantly to persuade herself that these people were not prisoners committed for the crime of lunacy. Weren't there bars on all the windows? And even the patients permitted out of doors were supervised and could not leave the grounds. In the afternoons they wandered about the hillside picking at things, like chickens. Or they sat immobile, hands clenched, on the benches, staring.

She could not regard them as the others did. The others astonished her. She had read somewhere, once long ago, that the staffs of mental hospitals were little more rational than the inmates, and were largely composed of sadists, perverts, misfits of all kinds. And in a way, this nonsensical idea struck her as more plausible than the selflessness she had come upon at Lime Rock Hospital. Yes, they were an ill-assorted lot, eccentric, even, some of them, but weren't the saints eccentric? It required a sort of saint, she thought, to work in a place like this for next to nothing, to rise above repulsion and sometimes fear, to love these mismade, badly broken creatures.

For in their separate ways, however tough or cynical or morbid, these people loved the patients. No other word described their attitude. Even the student nurses, younger than Anne and giggling, were finally seized by the same devotion, though chronic sufferers from nervous strain. As Mac had once remarked to Anne, "Even the veteran people here need a good, long weekend off now and again, but they come back."

I'd never come back, Anne had thought at the time. If I were weak enough to quit, I'd never find strength to return. But now, through Ernest Hamlin, she was nearing involvement in her work, and with it the dedication which sustained the others. She refused to be frightened off by Harry Marvin.

Anne sought out Dr. Sobel, who glanced over Hamlin's record. "What the patient has told you is true," Dr. Sobel started. "It's also true that he recognizes certain symptoms in advance, and reports them, so that these attacks can be to a certain extent controlled. But it isn't only a matter of recurrent pain, as he believes —"

"He's rational, then, Dr. Sobel, he's perfectly sane."

"Legally, perhaps. But apart from the pain he suffers —"

She didn't want to hear it. She said, "Then I think you should recommend that he be released in the custody of his doctor."

Dr. Sobel raised his eyebrows in alarm, clearly as surprised as she at her new candor. "I haven't the authority, Anne. And even if I had, I wouldn't use it."

"But you've just finished saying —"

"You won't let me finish," he said to her, smiling, and when she sat back in her chair, continued gently, "The fact remains that he has scraps of metal in the neural tissue. An operation is virtually out of the question. And that tissue may deteriorate."

"Well, until it does, I think he ought to be an out-patient. You say yourself that he reports the symptoms, and therefore isn't dangerous. You say —"

"He reports them today. But tomorrow? He's unpredictable, you see, and therefore must be regarded as mentally ill. He might get a crucial knock on the head, or his personality might change entirely. The possibilities extend from idiocy to death. We just can't tell as yet."

"Does he know this?"

"Yes. I took his word for it that he wanted to know. He's a courageous man. But he can't believe it yet, poor fellow, and perhaps that's just as well."

Anne stared at him, still struggling with his previous remark. "I can't believe it myself," she whispered. "He's so normal, so healthy. He's healthier than I am."

Dr. Sobel parried her gaze with the shield of official jargon. "The hospital couldn't accept responsibility for his release," he said, and fingered his Phi Beta Kappa key.

Rising, she said, as if in afterthought. "And isn't it a more serious responsibility not to take a chance but to keep a patient here unfairly?"

"Half the patients here are here unfairly, Anne. You yourself must know a dozen people now at large who might replace those in your ward. Some of our eccentric old people, some of the children, some of the retarded — there'd be places for all of them in secure or unselfish homes. There's no place for Hamlin in any home."

She ran into Harry Marvin outside. It was almost as if he had determined to follow her around, to badger her. He apologized for his rudeness, however, and displayed concern about what Dr. Sobel had had to say.

"That's right," he said, when she had finished. "This is a state hospital, and state appointees must place their responsibilities to the public, the voting public, that is, above the fate of this individual, this unimportant individual. Mental hospitals are a bum investment, they don't pay off politically, as Mac says."

"What do you mean, unimportant individual? Didn't he fight for his country? Isn't that why he's here? How can you say —"

"You're very young, Anne, and very naive. Nobody in Lime Rock is important, politically or otherwise, or they wouldn't be here. This man Hamlin of yours is an ex-machinist. If he was an ex-alderman, the son of an ex-alderman, or knew the son of an ex-alderman, or even an ex-policeman, he'd be at home, at least until he hurt somebody."

"I don't believe it!"

"I can't help it if you don't. But it's the truth. There's a kid in the Monkey House who's only here because he was *born* here, how do you like that? To a schizo prostitute who died. Who's going to speak up for him? I looked into it, and I got the story that the foundling homes are already overcrowded, and that he might as well be left here until he's old enough to go to school. By that time he will probably be very well qualified to stay right where he is."

"You just looked into it, is that it? You didn't try to do anything about it."

"As a matter of fact, I did. But not too hard. I didn't risk losing my job over it, and that's because there are too few of us willing to work here. Trained people, that is," he added, pointedly. "In other words, I'm no use to these people if I'm outside."

"I wish I had your self-confidence," Anne snapped, outraged.

"Oh, you'll have it," Harry said, "when you've been here a little while." He glided effortlessly over her sarcasm. "And I'm glad to see you taking such an interest in a patient, by the way. Do you really care what happens to him?"

"Yes, I do. I admire him. I told him I'd try to help him, and I will."

"You *told* him that?"

"Yes, I did."

"You've made a bad mistake."

"I know I have," Anne said. She fled before the tears came.

"Never mind Harry," Mac told her later. "He's fine with those children, and he works very hard, but he's a little nervous about his importance here. That's why he takes it out on you, I think. He's possessive about the place, for some reason. In fact, just between you and me, he's goddamned neurotic and no mistake." She jammed her cigarette into her coffee cup. "We all are, I guess. The longer you work here the more clearly you recognize the very fine line between ourselves and the patients. Sometimes there's no line at all, or rather, people cross it, back and forth, back and forth, from both sides. When you see that, and see that mental illness is largely a matter of degree, then you can identify yourself with the patients, and work with all your heart."

Anne nodded. "I think I know what you mean, now, after talking to Ernest Hamlin."

"Perhaps you do," Mac said shortly. Her statement of faith of a moment before had made her uncomfortable. "The other thing that I wanted to say to you was that Harry Marvin was right — you *have* made a mistake. But we've all made that mistake here when our emotions got involved. It only happens to you once. It takes just once to learn. So forget it."

Anne nodded again. "And you can't help him either, Mac?"

"I'll give it a try," Mac said.

She went to see the Director. "I tried," she reported to Anne the following day. "Old Silvertongue said he understood the unhappy predicament of the patient, but that his own hands were tied. He said this Hamlin was committed through the Veteran's Hospital, that it might be called a federal affair. He also said that, while of course he was grateful for my services, I might reflect on the fact that I have no medical training and am hardly in a position to contest the decision of qualified doctors. He set me straight, in short." Mac shrugged her shoulders. "Give it up, kid. Life's too short to get angry about injustice, in this place or out of it. Sobel's Augean Stable is the world. I've been angry since I came here, fifteen years ago, and all I've got to show for it is ulcers."

Ernest Hamlin came every day to the Occupational Therapy Unit and worked unceasingly with the other patients. At first they resented what they considered to be presumption on the part of their fellow sufferer, soon they came to depend on him, and were cross and quarrelsome during two days when he did not come. Anne did not ask him where he had been, nor did she have to, since his haggard face told her all she needed to know. And he only said, smiling, "That was kind of a bad one," en route to a discussion of grandchildren with a hazy old woman who did not realize that these very grandchildren of whom she was so proud had seen to it that she would end her days at Lime Rock State Mental Hospital.

Unlike Anne, Ernest could make these people laugh. She could not quite understand how he went about it, except that he made of himself a sort of gift, a plaything. He was their friend and confessor, but he was also their scapegoat, shuffleboard victim, and willing butt of their strange humor. The room rang with cries of "Ernie, Ernie!", as if only he, like a big blond Peter Pan, could bring to life their makeshift games.

Anne, too, now enjoyed her work, she, too, depended on him. She took such pleasure in his company that at times she forgot or put aside the remembrance that he was waiting for her help. For though he never once mentioned her offer or alluded to it, she sensed that his happy efforts with the patients were in part inspired by the possibility of his own deliverance, a possibility held out by Anne and Anne alone, and that he had to struggle to keep from questioning her about her progress.

And of course she had made no progress, had, in fact, given up. Once, in exasperation at her helplessness, she had tried to parcel out the burden of her blame. "What about your mother?" she had said to Ernie. "Does she come to visit you?"

He had been uncomfortable. "No," he said, and after a moment, "The trip is kind of hard for her. She's kind of old and she ain't got too much money, see, and — I don't know, to tell you the honest-to-God truth. I thought maybe she might make it up here once or twice, but she didn't."

"But your fiancee — wouldn't she come if you wrote to her? Or at least encourage your mother to come if she couldn't come herself."

"No, not her. She'd do just the opposite, I guess. If Ma comes, she's got to come, too, or else feel bad about not coming. She ain't mean or nothing, only a little selfish, just between you and me."

"But I thought you were in love with her."

"No, I never said that. I kind of *had* to marry her, for old time's sake, because of the way we were before I went to Korea." He blushed, and blushing, added, "After knowing you, I couldn't marry her no more anyway."

She had guessed already that he thought himself in love with her, and she in turn admired him, depended on him, yes, and "loved" him, if that were the same thing. So now they faced each other, breathless.

"Thanks," said her voice, too loudly, jauntily. "You're not so bad yourself." She had inherited her mother's habit of turning beet red in the face. Later she told herself that she had flirted with him selfishly, thus compounding her earlier crime.

"Ernie," she said another day, determined to have it out with him, "there's nothing I can do to help you. I've talked to people, and the Director knows about it, even, and they all say the same thing — it has to be worked through the Veteran's Hospital."

She could not bear to look at his face until he spoke. "Anne, I told you that before, I told you there ain't nothing you can do." His voice was unnaturally calm. She peered at him. He was trying to smile, but some vital element was dying in his face, shifting and fading like the bright colors of a fish. He stood transfixed before her, unaware of a shrill voice from across the room.

"Ernie, Ernie, come play shuffleboard! Ernie, Ernie!"

She started to cry, and he came forward and took her hand.

"Why am I crying?" she mumbled, enraged at herself. "I'm being so silly, Ernie. You just have to write that hospital and ask for a review of your case, that's all . . ."

"That's all," Ernie said.

" . . . . and it won't be long before they develop some safe new operating technique, you'll be out of here in no time." She wiped her eyes and attempted a cheerful smile.

"That's right," Ernie said.

She had never seen such an expression in her life.

She plunged onward, hopelessly. "And you've got to be careful in the meantime, Ernie, not to bump your head, you've got to have patience and courage."

"How did you know about my head?" Ernie said.

"Dr. Sobel. You've got to be very careful, you've got to —"

"Dr. Sobel. He's okay, Dr. Sobel," Ernie nodded his head. "Thanks anyway. I'll see you later."

"Where are you going?"

"Don't you hear them calling to me? I'm going to play shuffleboard with the boys."

"Ernie!"

He waited.

"Ernie, everything's going to work out fine! And afterwards, maybe you and I, we can celebrate together —"

She saw that instant that she had made still another mistake. Instead of cheering him, she had made him face the facts, Dr. Sobel's facts, and his face quivered on the point of tears. He turned and fled, and she did not talk to him again.

Anne found a student nurse to take her place. She went for a walk between the rufous buildings, driven faster and faster until she found herself running, going nowhere. The day was cold, it was nearly December now, and the sharp air seared her lungs.

Afterwards, Ernie came more rarely to her ward. When he did come, he avoided her, and she did not seek him out. She had only worsened things with every effort to assist him, and was frightened of her own ineptitude. Yet she watched him, and when he imagined she was not looking he watched her. He helped with the patients less and less, and they in turn called out to him less, as if they now included him in their ranks and meant to treat him with the same suspicion and superiority with which, unpersuaded of their own conditions, they treated the other sick around them. Only once she went to him and asked him how he felt, and he said shortly, "I feel dandy." In the way that, once, his presence in the ward had given her confidence, it now inhibited her.

She was startled by her new assertive self, the self that stood up to Harry Marvin, tried to bully Dr. Sobel, coerced poor Mac into visiting the Director. True, it had brought her confidence when she needed it most, and she had Ernest Hamlin to thank for this. But it had also betrayed her into errors she would never before have had the courage to approach.

Harry Marvin was right, she told herself. I don't belong here.

One night early in December she was awakened by the telephone, and made her way downstairs to answer it. "We need everyone out here, Anne," came Harry's voice, trying not to sound excited. "We've got an emergency on our hands."

"I'll be right there," Anne said aloud, although he had hung up already.

It was nearly midnight.

On the highway by the main gate were a number of cars with motors running. A state policeman held up a white gloved hand in the beam of her headlights.

"Authorized personnel only, Miss."

"I'm a volunteer worker here. They telephoned me."

Their voices were loud in a noise like heavy wind. He consulted a list.

"No Pryor listed, Miss. Authorized personnel only. You better move your car, Miss, you're blocking the entrance."

"Officer, they need people up there, they telephoned me —"

"C'mon, girlie, I told you once, no sightseers, no visitors. I got my orders! Now let's move along!"

"I'm not a sightseer! I work here, I really do!" Anne's voice broke, she was shaking with nervousness and cold, as a second angry officer came forward and Mac drew up alongside.

"McKittredge, Miss Adelaide," Mac barked, seeing the list. "What's the matter, Anne?"

The second officer said, "Oh, Jesus," and waved Anne after Mac. She drove haltingly through the milling faces, which were shouting above the din, a din which rose out of the night time behind the trees. Then she traced Mac's blood red tail lights, which cut up the hill into the darkness like two fast angry insects. Her heart moved violently, and she felt sick.

There were lights in the Administration Building but the other shapes crouched back into the night. People ran in all directions. "They've cut the lights," Mac shouted in Anne's ear. She had a cigarette stub in her mouth, trotting clumsily along the driveway.

"What's happening, what's happening!" Anne cried, her voice picked up and whirled away in the avalanche of noise, a noise of endless feet in flight across a waste of concrete, of objects smashed against high iron windows, a noise of screaming.

The sound ricocheted around among the buildings, breaking out to surge like wind along the barren hillside, down across the frozen winter woods, the highway and the town beyond.

Anne was sent with a student nurse to help in the Children's Ward. They ran together over the bare ground, forsaking the cement sidewalks.

"What's happening!" Anne cried again. "What's happening!"

"Rioting!" the girl shrieked back at her. "It started in the Men's Wards and spread all over!" The girl was beside herself with excitement, yet apparently unafraid. "We've got the doors locked, though, they can't get out, but they're breaking everything, the Director says, he's getting the fire trucks up here with fire hoses!"

The Children's Wards were nearly under control. The children had been herded into corners. Most of them were badly frightened, and some of these were hysterical and screaming. A few were still running wild, hurling clothes and toothbrushes and bedpans; one little boy kicked furiously at an idiot huddled by the broken window. A big nurse reached him and he cursed and struck at her. Like most of the others he was naked in the winter draughts which swept the room. This little boy was named Robert Esposito, and he still bore scars inflicted by his father before and after he had finally set fire to his school.

Anne went from there to the Women's Wards. Here, too, the worst of the riot was over, and she wondered fleetingly if she would ever find a chance to be of use. The clothes of the women had been ripped to pieces, and they wandered aimless in their nudity, complaining. One was in a catatonic state and had attached herself, in frenzy, to another. The victim was a nice old woman known as Happy who was sent lollipops from home. She suffered a slight heart attack as the other woman was pried from her, and helping the frail body to a bed, Anne smelled the forsaken age of her and knew at last the love for these patients that the others felt. "Ah, dearie, thank you," the old woman gasped. "It isn't fit for folks like us to see such terrible sights, and I thank the Good Lord that my children never will."

By five in the morning, the Men's Wards had been subjugated. The midnight dark was turning towards a winter gray. Anne, standing in the cold, smoked a solitary cigarette and wondered about Ernest Hamlin. Before her the fire trucks, red lights still flashing, backed across the frozen earth, and the hoses nosed through the end doors of the buildings. The men inside were shouting still and pounding the bars on the upper floors, but the cries were more protesting now and less excited. The roar sagged slowly to a fretful moan and finally to a whine, until only now and then a minor metal object clanked without spirit on the bars, and the water pumps on the fire trucks commandeered the silence of December dawn. She learned from Harry later that an old man named Herbie Collins had been hurled against the wall by the rush of water and had died within minutes of a fractured skull.

"Poor old Collins staggered into the way," Harry Marvin said, "but that hose was aimed at your friend Ernest Hamlin." Harry was drawn and in need of a shave, and upset about Robert Esposito, who had been making progress, Harry said, considering the fact that twice before being sent to Lime Rock he had been hospitalized after discipline by his father.

They were having coffee in the basement of the Administration Building.

"Why Ernest?" Anne said.

"Because he started the whole business. The guy with the hose didn't know that, of course, he only saw that this big ox with the plumbing pipe in his hand and pounding his head against the wall was the man to stop. That's why."

"How is he?"

"Who?"

"Ernie."

"I don't know how Ernie is. I don't care how Ernie is, either. I care about Robert Esposito and poor old Collins."

"He's hurt himself," Dr. Sobel told her, and his interruption was a clear rebuke to Harry. He had been silent until now and staring at his coffee. "Hamlin had an attack, and he didn't give us warning. I think he knew he was going to have it. I think he hit his head on purpose. But," he said to Harry Marvin, "I don't think he started the riot on purpose. I think he frightened the others and got them excited."

"That's right," another doctor said. "I talked to one of my patients in there. He said this Hamlin started yelling, that he got into the washroom and wrenched this pipe loose and started breaking things. Then the men in his ward got excited and started yelling for help, and the other wards just sort of picked it up. Of course certain patients joined Hamlin in pounding on the bars and breaking, it was a release for them in a way, and finally the whole place was infected. Like a plague."

"Where is he now?" Anne whispered.

"We have him under pheno-barb," a nurse said briskly. "He's upstairs right now, in the In-Patients Room. But we're transferring him to the Disturbed Ward."

"He's going to stay there, too," Harry Marvin said.

"He's hurt himself. I don't know why, but he's hurt himself. On purpose." Dr. Sobel tapped a small sad finger on his temple. "Probably permanently. I've talked to him already."

"Did he hurt anybody else?"

"No," Harry Marvin snapped. "That's one thing he didn't do. He was much too normal, as you know, to do anything like that."

"Harry," Mac said, "Why don't you shut up?" She got to her feet and left the room, and Anne followed her.

44

"I'd like to see him, Mac," she said.

Mac nodded approvingly.

"Good for you, go right ahead. He's receiving, as you know, in the In-Patients Room. Poor bastard." She banged through the Supply Room door.

Anne climbed the stairs and went to see Ernest Hamlin. His head was on a pillow, bandaged, and his body was strapped to the metal cot. When she entered the room, he opened his eyes and constructed a sort of smile.

"I made it, kid," he said. "The varsity shuffleboard team." He started to laugh, a laughter high like crying. Then he frowned. "They hurt me in there. I told you they were out to get me because I wasn't nuts like them, and now they hurt me. My head hurts, see. They knew it was dangerous for me to hurt my head, and they hurt me anyway!"

He seemed surprised.

"Who, Ernie?" She wanted to reach out to him but could not. Through the window behind him she could see the fringe of trees down to the east, etched black by the sharp rising light of winter sun, and she thought, Beyond there, far away, the outside world encircles us, and pins us in.

"They. Those guys. All those guys."

"The doctors, you mean? The firemen?"

"Yeah, everybody," Ernest Hamlin muttered. "Them, too. All those guys." He was staring straight at the white ceiling, frowning, and took no notice of her when she bent and pressed her forehead to the cool iron of his cot.

Saturday Evening Post
September 28, 1963

LATE IN THE SEASON

It was just at the edge of the late November road, a halted thing too large for the New England countryside, neither retreating nor pulling in its head, but waiting for the station wagon. Cici Avery saw it first, a dark giant turtle, as solitary as a misplaced object, or something left behind after its season. She nudged her husband and pointed, unwilling to break the silence in the car.

Frank Avery saw the turtle and slowed. If he had been alone, he would have swerved to hit it, Cici decided, selecting the untruth which suited her mood.

The small eyes reflected the slowing car, then fastened on the man. The tail, ridged with reptilian fins, lay still in the dust like a thick dead snake, pointing to the yellowed weeds which, leading back over a slight crest and descending thickly to the ditch, were flattened and coated by a wake of mud.

Cici, hands in her trousers, moved in unlaced boots past her husband. The tips of the laces flicked in the dust like broken whip ends.

"Poor monster," she whispered to the turtle, "it's late in the year for you, you're past your season."

"Monster isn't the word," Frank Avery said. "I've never seen such a brute." He ventured a thrust at it with his riding boot. "It's not *really* a turtle?" he said.

"A snapping turtle," Cici said. She was a big untidy girl, whose straw-colored hair blurred the lines of her face.

"A man-eater," he said. "It must be two feet across."

"It's a very big old monster," she said, sinking down on the crest behind it and stroking the triangular snout with her stick. The mouth reared back over the shell, its jaws slicing the stick with a leathery thump.

"Dear God!" Frank said.

Cici eased to her elbow in the grass, stretching the long legs in faded hunting pants out to one side of the turtle, and studied her husband. Frank Avery, precise in his new riding habit, stood uncertain beside the bull-like turtle, afraid of it and fascinated at once.

The very way he behaves with me, the thought recurred to her, as if I were some slightly disgusting animal, and yet he prides himself on his technique. The father of my children, except that his technique doesn't include having children. Romance is the watchword, but no children, not for a while. And then he is hurt because I don't love him. As if we were haggling over love as the stud fee, as if I had bargained with him for his manhood, she thought, and didn't realize until I took it home what a rotten bargain I had made.

Frank Avery stretched out his toe and sent the turtle sprawling on its back.

"Come on, you coward," he challenged it. "Fight."

The turtle reached back into the dust with its snout and pivoted itself upright with its neck muscles, then heaved around to face the enemy.

"Leave it alone," Cici said. "It can't help being a turtle."

"We should kill it," Frank told her. "It's disgusting."

We should kill it, she thought, because it's harmful on a farm, not for *your* reason. Lying there watching him badger the turtle, she felt a slow hurt anger crawling through her lungs, as if he had injured her over a period of time and only now she understood. She was sorry for the turtle, for its mute acceptance of the riding boots which barred its way.

"You don't have to look at it," she said. "Besides, it's mine. I saw it first."

He turned to her, hands on hips, smiling his party smile.

"A fine thing," he said, and waited for her question.

"What is?" she obliged him, after a moment.

"Here we've only been married a year and now it's turtles. First it was kittens and puppies, and then horses, and now turtles. I appreciate your instincts, Cici, but you *can't* get weepy over turtles!"

He laughed sharply.

"Can't I?" she said. Unsmiling, she waited for the laugh to wither in his mouth.

Frank kicked suddenly at the turtle's head, but his toe shrank from the contact and only arched a wave of dust into the hard stretched mouth and the little eyes. When the turtle blinked, the dust particles fell from above its eyelids.

"Did I ever tell you about Toby Snead, Frank? When the other kids would torture a rat or a frog, Toby Snead would jump around, squealing and giggling. He loved it. He was skinny and weak, and he loved to see them pick on something besides himself."

"Was I giggling?" Frank said. His face was white.

I've gone too far, Cici thought, and I'm going to go farther. She felt exhausted, lying back in the natural grass, easing herself of a year of disappointment as calmly as a baby spitting up cereal, a little startled at the produce of its mouth, yet more curious than concerned.

"And you'll get your shiny new manly boots dirty, Frank," she murmured.

"I haven't been here every year to get them faded," he said. When she didn't answer, he added, "And pick up a local accent, and ogle the hired hand."

"The caretaker, you mean," Cici said, her eyes on the turtle. He's jealous, she thought, actually jealous; he can't admit that *he* made a rotten bargain, too.

"Oh Cici, let's skip it," Frank said. "I don't know what's the matter with you these days."

"I hope you find out," Cici said, turning her eyes on him, "before my change of life."

"Let's not start *that* all over again," Frank Avery said. His voice was tight, a little desperate. "I'm sick of it. And you'll catch cold, sitting on the ground."

"There's plenty between me and the ground," Cici said, grinning. She rose and, turning her buttocks to him, brushed the grass off with both hands.

"See?" she said, over her shoulder. "Besides, I've got *you* to keep me warm."

She stepped around the turtle and, taking Frank's face between her hands, kissed him with exaggerated sensuality on the mouth. When he tried to embrace her, however, she slipped from him.

"Cici, listen to me," he said, but she refused, stooping to the turtle.

"C'mon, monster," she said. "I'll take you home and mother

you."

"Permit me," Frank said, and clowned a bow, but his heart was not in it. Circling behind the turtle, he seized it convulsively by the rear edges of its carapace and bore it like a hot unbalanced platter to the car.

"What do you want him for?" he said. Then, "Open the door, will you?"

"Monster's peeing on you," Cici told him, laughing in a way which suggested an alliance with the turtle against him. Watching his face, she was sorry she had laughed, but not for Frank's sake. Frank was an artist at revenge, he much preferred it to the messy temper which came to Cici so naturally. She knew him now, and she could expect reprisal with as much confidence as she had in his execution of it.

The turtle blundered to the rear of the station wagon and pressed its snout against the backboard. It seemed alarmed by this detour in its life, scraping its claws like harsh fingernails over the metal floor.

"Let's let it go, Frank," Cici said, afraid.

"No, no," Frank insisted. "I'm sure Cyrus would like to see it." He was smiling.

Indoors, the turtle looked double its size. Cyrus Jone's boy Jackie had never seen anything like it. He trapped the turtle in the kitchen corner and dropped marbles on its head until Cici asked him to stop. Mrs. Jone, thin-armed in a cotton print, rushed over and slapped him in deference to Mrs. Avery.

Cyrus nodded shortly at Cici as if to excuse his remark, and said to his wife, "Not much sense in slappin' the boy if you ain't spoken to him first. He ain't a dog."

"I can't have him pesterin' folks, " she whined, retreating to the stove.

Cyrus Jone did not answer her. He said to Cici, "Your father telephoned, Miss Cici, he's comin' down tomorrow."

"Oh, that'll be nice," squeaked Mrs. Jone.

"Yes," Cici said. She was holding a baby Jone on her lap while its mother, one eye on the turtle, rummaged nervously with the supper.

Jackie, a large-headed child with prominent ears, goaded the turtle furtively. It renewed its effort to penetrate the corner.

"That's enough, Jackie," his father told him.

"I ain't doin' nothin'," the boy said, injured. "I just wanted to see if he was all right."

"He's all right," Cyrus said. He was a big man of strong middle age, whose hands rested tranquilly on his knees. His eyes were restless, however, and Cici knew he was watching her from the shadow of his corner; she glanced at his wife, already pressing a new round belly to the stove.

Frank Avery came into the kitchen. In his left hand he carried a .22 pistol, which he placed in the corner of the sideboard, in his right the whisky bottle from their suitcase. It was not quite full, Cici noticed.

"I'll have your dinner in a minute, Mr. Avery," Mrs. Jone said. Her eyes switched rapidly from the bottle to the turtle to the pistol, coming to rest at last on Frank's forehead.

"Why don't we all eat together?" Cici said.

"And Cici can hold the baby," Frank said to her.

Cici did not return his smile, and only Jackie said,

"Sure, we kin all eat together and watch the turtle."

"That's right," Frank said. "We might have a cocktail before-hand."

"I'm sure you folks'd rather . . . " Mrs. Jone began, terrified.

"What are you gonna do with the pistol?" Jackie demanded, touching it.

He's been drinking upstairs, Cici thought, I'll never placate him now, and I've missed my chance to let the turtle go. She had forgotten the turtle, she knew it did not matter to her, but suddenly its survival seemed urgent.

"Whatever you folks want'll do fine for us," Cyrus said. He rapped his fingers on his knees.

"Hey, what are you gonna do with the pistol?" Jackie repeated.

"Mr. Avery," Mrs. Jone corrected him.

"Mister Avery," Jackie said.

But Frank had gone to the pantry for ice. He returned in a moment with four glasses of it.

"Great," he said, pouring out the whisky.

In the moment of silence, the turtle pushed upward against the wall, then fell back heavily to the floor.

"Jackie wants to know what you're going to do with the pis-tol," Cici said.

"I was just about to ask Cyrus," Frank said. He passed the glasses and sat down.

"What's that, Mr. Avery?" Cyrus said.

"That turtle, Cyrus. I understand that kind of turtle is harmful, eats fish and young ducks and things."

"Frogs, mostly. That's right, though."

"Dangerous to swimmers, I imagine."

"I don't guess so. They're pretty leary, them hogbacks."

"Frank wants to kill the turtle, Cy," Cici said.

"Sure, let's kill'm!" Jackie said. "We kin shoot him with the pistol."

"Shush, Jackie," hissed Mrs. Jone. When Cici glanced at her, she hid her whisky glass among the pots on the back of the stove.

"I don't *want* to kill it, darling," Frank said. "I just don't think we should let it go."

"That's too bad, *dar*ling," Cici told him. "Because it's my turtle. I found it, and I'm going to let it go."

Her anger was sudden and quiet. The little boy watched her, open-mouthed, and Cyrus said,

"I guess I'd ha' killed it, had I found it, Miss Cici."

"You didn't find it, though," Cici snapped.

"You're being childish about it, Cici," Frank interrupted.

"No, I didn't, that's true," Cyrus laughed, as if Frank's remark were of no more consequence than the turtle's bumping in the corner. "But there's not much good in a critter like that."

"That's right," Frank Avery said. Prematurely, he refilled all the glasses but Cici's, which was untouched, and now sat down again. "We all agree it should be killed, Cici."

"I ain't sayin' *that*," Cyrus said. "I don't guess one turtle could do much harm on a place this size, although I'd just as soon be rid of it."

The baby was stirring now in Cici's arms.

"I'll take it upstairs," Cici said, over the protests of Mrs. Jone. Her face, pressed to the baby's head, softened again to its usual fullness, but her mouth was set, and she did not look at her husband as she rose.

"Cici loves babies," Frank's voice said, pursuing her to the back stairway; it was followed by a laugh. "Babies and turtles."

Mrs. Jone's giggle tinkled like the cheap alarm clock over the pots on the stove.

She was still giggling when Cici returned and sat down to dinner.

"I *do* love babies, yes," Cici said to Frank.

"Well, I must say they're a terrible trouble," Mrs. Jone told her. "You don't know your own luck, Mrs. Avery."

"We have a baby every year," Jackie announced, but his mouth was already so occupied that nobody understood him except his mother.

She said, "Jackie!" and blushed.

Cyrus watched his wife, chewing his dinner without expression.

The turtle had found its way out of the corner and was dragging itself along the wall in the direction of the kitchen door. Cici listened. The belly plate touched the floor on alternate steps, a dull pendulum rhythm of tap and suspense which went unnoticed at the table.

"Yes, they'd certainly be trouble in *my* work, with all the traveling I do," Frank was saying.

"Oh, you'll have them, though, Mr. Avery," said Mrs. Jone. "Never you fear. Why, it's only nature."

"It's only nature, Frank," Cici grinned.

"Of course we will," Frank Avery frowned. Unlike Mrs. Jone, he had brought his whisky to the table. "Right now, of course, it's inconvenient, but there's plenty of time. We're only thirty."

Cici did not comment, she had heard it all before, and to her it rang false and unnatural. Her time growing shorter, she had settled for Frank Avery and children. She had wanted to love him so badly, and now, in secret ways, he punished her failure. And having settled for less, she was to be cheated even of what she had settled for. It was all Cici could do to swallow, and sorry for herself, she permitted her eyes to cloud with tears.

She wondered if Catholic Mrs. Jone had been offended by his tactlessness. But Mrs. Jone was obviously too stimulated to be offended by anything, and Cici looked at Cyrus, who was now intent on the turtle's progress along the wall.

Very quietly, without turning toward her, Cyrus said,

"His pond must have dried out on him, he's after a new mud to winter in, this late in the year."

Cici nodded. The turtle had exposed itself to trouble.

She watched her husband, who had heard Cyrus' voice but lost the words in the clatter of Jackie's fork, and was now glancing from one to the other with a half-smile, as if he wished to be enlightened.

The turtle was directly behind him.

Cici did not enlighten her husband, but offered instead a wink of innocence and duplicity which brought new color to his face. He glared expectantly at Cyrus, but Cyrus was absorbed with his mashed potatoes and did not notice.

Frank rose abruptly and went into the pantry for more ice.

Moving quickly, Cici horsed the turtle over the floor and out the kitchen door into the darkness, straining the precious seconds in her effort to be quiet.

"Oh boy," Jackie said, rising. "Let's go!"

"Be quiet," his father told him, his eyes on Frank Avery, who returned as Cici sat down. Frank's face was red with irritation, and he only glanced at her questioningly.

Cici smiled at him and said nothing. Her heart pounding, she cheered the turtle toward the bushes. The success of her coup was overpowering: like a schoolgirl, she was forced to bite on the insides of her cheeks to keep from laughing, trembling joyfully in the escape as in a childhood game of hide-and-seek.

"But it'll get away," Jackie whispered to his father, turning away sharply as if he hadn't meant to whisper it, it had just popped out, and therefore he was not to be blamed.

"My mashed potatoes are quite nice and fluffy tonight, if I *do* say so," preened Mrs. Jone, and dropped her fork.

"But listen . . . " Jackie started.

Frank shifted his gaze to Cyrus, who, chewing placidly, returned it.

"When we're finished dinner," Frank said to Jackie, "we'll have to kill the turtle."

"I'm finished now," Jackie blurted. "It's going to get away."

And then there was silence. Finally, Frank Avery said, "Where in hell did it get to, Cici?"

"I let it go." The laughter jerked from her mouth.

"The turtle?" Mrs. Jone said. She stared at the empty corner.

"That was silly of you, Cici," Frank said. He was trying to control his voice. "You knew it should have been killed."

"Oh, relax, Frank," she said. "It doesn't matter."

"It *does* matter, damn it."

They watched him rise and take the pistol and, followed by Jackie, step out into the darkness.

"Jackie," his mother said.

Cici rose and went to the door. "Frank," she called.

He came back into the light. "I need a flashlight," he muttered. Behind him, Jackie's voice rang through the darkness.

"Frank, don't. Please," she whispered. "It was mine. You're just killing it to spite me."

"You shouldn't have let it go," he said, pushing past her. "You've tried to make a fool of me all day."

When he came back through the kitchen, Cyrus watched him without speaking, but Mrs. Jone whispered,

"It's only just a turtle, everybody. Your dinner'll get cold."

Frank grinned tightly, saying to Cyrus, "We shouldn't let it go."

In the door, Cici blocked his way.

"You're being ridiculous, Frank. You're drunk. And who found the turtle? It's mine."

"God damn it," he said. "You knew I wanted that turtle killed."

"Why?" she demanded, her whisper harsh as the turtle's sigh. "Why? Since when are you so interested in ducks and fish and things? They've kept going pretty well so far without any help from you, or the little boy you drag in to keep your courage up."

"You know . . . " he started, but did not bother to go on, because Jackie had found the turtle.

Defeating its own escape, it was pushing against the center of the nearest bush, its legs braced in the dirt; from the doorway, Cici saw Frank's dark hand reach across the flashlight beam and grasp the spiny tail.

Sick, she turned back into the kitchen. When Cyrus rose and went out, she snapped at Mrs. Jone,

"How can you sit there and let that little boy watch him?"

Mrs. Jone ran outside.

The shots came slow and unevenly—one, twothree, four. The fourth shot drove Cici to the door.

The turtle was moving slowly in the dim light from the kitchen. Frank's back was to her, and through the excited shouts of the little boy and the shrilling of his mother, she heard a quieter sound.

"What are you laughing at?" she said, her voice hushed, but he was pointing the pistol again, leaning back, stiff-armed.

The turtle jerked a little, kept on moving away. One of its hind legs was paralyzed, and there were three black holes in the ancient shell.

"What are you laughing at?" Cici screamed, and the boy Jackie ran into the house after his mother.

"I'm sorry, darling," Frank's voice came. "I know it's not funny, but my shooting's terrible. I can't seem to hit its head."

"It's still moving," Cici whispered, as he turned to her. "You bastard. You perfect bastard."

"I'm sorry," he repeated, as if bewildered. "I must have been drunk." He put his hand to his forehead. "I didn't think you'd watch."

Cyrus came around the corner from the garage. He had a hatchet in his hand, and stopped the turtle with his boot. It opened its mouth, but could not close it again.

"Hell, mister, that's no way to kill a hogback," Cyrus said.

He bent and guillotined the turtle as Cici cried out.

The blood was black on the ground beneath the door light. Cyrus lobbed the head with its still-open mouth out of the light, then hoisted the carcass by the tail and, holding it away from him, moved toward the bushes. Its hind feet were still walking away.

Crying now, Cici slumped in the doorway. Frank Avery tried to approach her.

"It's still moving," she whispered, damning him with her horror. "You coward. And you couldn't even kill it."

"Cici, listen," he started.

"I hate you," Cici told him. "You're disgusting."

The turtle fell in the invisible underbrush, a heavy breaking crash which jarred the night time into silence.

The returning steps of Cyrus Jone came from the darkness before them. Behind, the bright-lit kitchen waited, the empty chairs at angles to the cooling dinner. From an upper room, the little boy was crying.

New World Writing No. 3
1953

TRAVELIN MAN

November on the Carolina coast is cold at night, a dark clear cold that kills the late mosquitoes.

Toward dusk, a black man slithered from a drainage ditch. He moved swiftly on his belly, writhing out across a greasy bog and vanishing into the sawgrass by the river. The grass stirred a moment and was still. A rail bird rattled nervously, and a hunting gull, drawn inland, cocked a bright, hard, yellow eye. Startled, it dropped a white spot on the brown waste of the bog and banked downwind.

Deep River is dark with piedmont silt and without depth or bottom. It bends its way to its wide delta like a great dead snake slung out across the tidewater, and in the summertime it smells. Alluvial ooze packed tight and rotting on its banks sucks into itself the river debris. Through the grasses near the rim, Traver could see the stranded tree limbs and the prow of the derelict skiff glimpsed earlier in the day.

It was nearly dark. Raising his eyes to the level of the grass, he listened a last time. Then he slid forward and, on his knees in the shallows, wrenched the buried skiff from its sheath of mud. It came with a thick sucking sound and the rank breath of its grave.

Traver knew without experiment that, upright, the skiff would fill immediately. He turned it turtle and waited one moment more, gaining his wind. It was high water, the first of the ebb. The tide and river would be with him. He shivered, moaning softly, though not yet afraid.

In the water, he kicked away from shore. An eddy curled him back upon the bank. He kicked away a second time, and caught the current. But the slimy hulk would not support his weight, and he coasted along beside it, one hand spread-fingered on the keel.

He moved downstream. Across the marsh, the lights switched back and forth like night-time eyes, dancing in the blackness of the pines. The voices came vaguely on the shifting river air, and a new sound stirred him. He inched lower in the water, so that only his hand and half his face broke the low outline of the skiff.

Dey gone and put de hounds on dat man Traver.

He giggled, teeth chattering, and cursed.

The river dragged the capsized skiff across the coastal waterway, which parted the mainland from the inner marshes of the barrier islands. Though wisps of cloud at times obscured the moon, the night was clear. No longer able to see the lights, he was alone in the cold river, which widened now as it neared its mouth. He thrashed his legs for warmth, and cursed to restore his courage. Southeast, an arm of woods from Ocean Island reached across the outer marshes toward the bank. He wanted to go aground there, and fearful of drifting past it to the open sea, began to swim the skiff inshore. He swore foully at the balky hulk, the cold, the river, the night world, and then, despite himself afraid, he sang softly a song known long ago in the shanties of Raccoon Creek.

> Faraway and gone am I toward dat Judgment Day,
> Faraway and gone am I, ain't no one gwine to stay,
> Lay down dis haid, lay down dis load,
> Gwine to take dat Heaven Road,
> Faraway and gone am I toward dat Judgment Day.

His voice hung plaintive in the thin mist over the river, and startled by it, he had a cold premonition of his death. But an inshore current seized the skiff and swept it in beneath the bank. Nearing the piles of the abandoned landing, he forsook the skiff, and struggled through the shallow water. He had to drag himself ashore. Crouched beneath the wharf, too weak to beat his arms, he listened to hoarse, painful breaths he could not help. The skiff disappeared around the final bend, toward the booming where the seas broke on the bar.

Traver scraped coon oysters from the pilings and opened them with his knife. Since the clothes he wore were the property of the state, this knife was his sole possession. He had had it fifteen hours. The knife was long, with a spring blade, and when he had eaten, he cleaned it before replacing it in his pocket.

Then he rose, peering over the bank at the trees a hundred

yards away. Though sure he was alone on Ocean Island, he disliked outlining himself against the river. He went forward in a low crouch, covert, quiet. He liked to think he was quiet as an animal.

In the shelter of the live oaks, for the first time since early morning, he stood straight. Stretching, he threw his shoulders back, legs spread in unconsicous arrogance. Traver was a tall man and very strong, with the big hands and haunches of his race. His skin was the mud black of the coastal Gullah, and his left eye was obscured by scars which extended in cordy ridges toward the neat, tight ear. The scars seemed to have stretched the skin, which was taut and smooth, like a rubber mask. The expression of the mask was open, almost smiling, the boyish smile of a man enjoying himself without quite knowing why.

Most of the time, this smile was genuine. Traver liked to laugh and, though good-natured, he also liked to fight. He had been fighting since the day when, brought home to Raccoon Creek by a wayward mother, he was nicknamed Traveler.

> His Daddy was a Travelin Man
> Traveled away and left his Mam.

The name became Traver, and stayed with him. And he had traveled north, south, east, and west, in and out of work and jail. He could stay no longer in a job than out of trouble. He had worked on the railroad and the chain gang and the big menhaden boats out of Hampton Roads, and everywhere he laughed like hell and finally fought. Every once in a while, half-drunk, he would come home. And his mother would tell him, You born with too much life in you, dass all, you like you daddy. And you headin straight fo trouble, big mule as you is.

The last time home he had fought the man who happened to marry his girl. The man had knifed him near the eye. Unable to catch him, Traver, still bleeding, had burned their cabin down and taken the willing girl away. The sheriff followed in his own good time. I got your old place on the road gang saved for you, the sheriff said. We ain't had a good laugh since you left.

But now, a month later, he had escaped. He appeared with the knife in Raccoon Creek, but the man had moved away. The girl's mother reported him, and he took to the woods, and kept on going out across Deep River Marsh. The tide was flooding when he saw the skiff, and he had had to wait. He had scurried, crouched, scurried again, and once submerged, sliding beneath the surface like an alligator. They had not picked up his trail in the green, broken scum and, voices, rasping, they had passed.

I a big bull gator, he sang now, a tough-hide long-tail mean ol gator. Opening his open mouth a little more, he chortled sound-lessly, still shivering. It growin cold, and dis gator ain't no place to warm hisself. Well, I mean. Cold.

He moved inland through the trees, away from the dark river.

Ocean Island is long and large, spreading down some four miles from the delta, southwest toward Cape Romaine. The true land is a narrow spine supporting red cedar, cypress, yaupon, live oak, and the old-field pine, and here and there a scattering of small palmettos. There are low ridges and open groves and clearings, and a core of semi-tropic woods. Its south flank is salt marsh and ocean beach, and to the north, diked years ago above the tide, lies a vast, brackish swamp. The swamp is grassy, like a green-and-golden flooded plain, its distances broken by lone, bony trees and hurricane dikes and sluice gates. Here, in a network of overgrown canals, the nut and widgeon grass grows in abandoned rice fields. Wildfowl winter in a diadem of reedy ponds, and coot and rail and gallinule, and predators.

In the swamp, the predators move ceaselessly.

He went to Snake-house. This was a sagging tool shed near the landing, so-called because in other times a worker had been bitten there, and died. In the dark, a sign, NO TRESPASSING, loomed white and new. The door was gone, but the dank interior gave shelter from the breeze. Traver stripped and wrung his clothes, then rubbed his body fiercely with his hands. He found an oily piece of old tarpaulin, and wrapping himself in it, dozed a little, fitful.

He had come to Ocean Island because here he could survive. As a boy he had labored on the rice fields and the dikes, and he knew the name and character of every pond and ditch and slough. He knew where to snare rabbits, stalk birds, ambush deer, and where the wild swine and cattle were which he might outwit and kill. On the salt shores there were razor clams and oysters, and mullet in the canals, if a fish trap could be rigged. He would not starve. He could even eat raccoon and otter and, if necessary, he could eat them raw.

He could survive here, too, because he would not be caught. The island had been unused for years, even for gunning. If he were tracked to this forsaken place, he could always find shelter in the swamp. Hounds could not help them here, and the whites did not know the swamp as he did, how to move quickly in it without risking the deep potholes and soft muck. He could elude a wider search than the state would send into the swamp after a black man. For this was black man's country, slow and silent, absorbing the white man's inroads like a sponge. A white man loomed large on Ocean Island, but a black man was swallowed up in it, and disappeared.

In the night, he was awakened by the grunting of a hog. The grunt was nervous, and there was a skittish stamping of small, cloven hooves. He smell me, Traver thought. Taking his knife, he glided to the doorway. Upwind, the hog came toward him on the island path. He crouched, prepared to ambush it, then stiffened.

Ol Hawg scairt. And he ain't scairt of Traver.

Traver stooped for his shirt and pants and slipped outside. The hog snorted and wheeled, crashing off into the brush. Traver slid down a sand bank behind the Snake-house and lay watching. He heard a rush of bait fish by the landing, the choked cry of a night heron behind him. A barred owl stole over his head. This was the hunting time.

The man had not seen Traver. He had stopped short at the crashing of the hog. Now he came on, down the soft sand path towards Snake-house. He was a tall, lean man with a rifle slung over one arm and a flashlight, unlit, in the other hand. His face was shadowed in the moonlight by his hat brim, lowered all the way around.

Traver opened the knife blade and lay still. He could not retreat now without being seen, and if he was seen, he was lost. He had no doubt that this man was his enemy, an enemy as natural as a raccoon to a frog, nor did it occur to him to curse his luck that an enemy was here at all. He was only relieved that he had heard in time. The rest no longer mattered. Traver was hardened to hunting and being hunted, and the endless adaptation to emergencies. He was intelligent and resourceful, and he was confident. Through the grasses, he gauged the stranger as he passed.

From the man's belt, behind, hung a hatchet and a piece of rope. The rifle, carried loosely, was ready to be raised, and the unlit light was also ready. He was hunting. He crossed a patch of dry grass without a sound, and Traver nodded ruefully in respect.

Dat a poacher. Might be he jackin deer.

The man went on, down toward the landing. Stooping on the wharf, he peered beneath it. Traver, who had moved, could see him do this, and felt a tightening in his chest.

He see dem feet prints. He see white places where dem oyster was. You a plain fool nigger, man.

The hunter returned, moving more quickly. Raising his rifle, he flicked his light into the Snake-house. Traver could see its gleam through the rotting tongue-and-groove.

Ain't no deer in dar, Boss, ain't no deer in dar.

He repressed a nervous giggle, sweating naked in the cold, and clutched his knife. Upwind, he could hear the hog again, rooting stupidly near the path. The white man turned, bent to one knee, and fired. Traver jumped. The report ricocheted across the grove as the hog kicked, squealing, and lay still.

Ol white folks, he kin shoot. Only why he shootin now and not before? He lookin to fool somebody, he makin pretend he doan know somebody here.

He know, all right. Ol white folks know.

The man dragged the hog into the trees and dressed it quickly, viciously, with the hatchet and a knife. Then he piled brush on the head and hooves and entrails and, rigging a sling with a length of rope, hoisted the carcass to his shoulder. He went away as silently as he had come, and Traver followed.

We stickin close as two peas, man. I got to know what you up to every minute, lest you come sneakin up behind me.

Traver, though uneasy, was excited, jubilant. It seemed to him that he had won some sort of skirmish, and he could scarcely wait to see what would happen next. But because he guessed where the man was going, he kept a safe distance behind. There was a clearing at Back-of-Ocean, and the old cabin of an abandoned shooting camp, and the only beach on the south side steep enough to bring a boat ashore. The poacher would have to have a boat, and he probably had a helper. Realizing this, Traver slowed, and put on his wet clothes.

He circled the clearing and came in from the far side, on his belly. There was kerosene light in the cabin window, and hanging from its eaves on the outside logs were moonlit amorphous carcasses. He made out deer and pig, and what could only be the quarters of a large wild bull. These cattle gone wild were the wariest creatures on the island, and this sign of the hunter's skill gave him another start of uneasiness. Backing off again on hands and knees, he cut himself a rabbit club of the right weight. Waiting for dawn, he whittled it, and bound with vine and a piece of shirt two sharp stones to the heavy end. He was skillful with it, and the feel of it in his hand was reassuring.

It was growing light.

The boat appeared at sunup. Traver heard it a long way off, prowling the channel between islands at the southeast end. Now it drummed along the delta, just inside the bar, and headed straight in for the beach. It was a small, makeshift shrimp boat, with rust streaks and scaling gray-green paint. Before it grounded, the hunter came out and, hoisting two small deer onto his shoulders, went down to the shore.

The two men loaded quickly. Then they stood a moment talking, the one on the pale sand of the beach, the other a black silhouette on the bow against the red fireball of the sun.

For once in his life, Traver told himself, he had to stop fooling and be serious. The boatman, who must have been in town the night before, had probably confirmed whatever the hunter had noticed at the landing. He wondered if they would turn him in. He doubted it. In the prison denims, he could be shot on sight, and no questions asked—not that the hunter would require that excuse. He guessed that the latter had some right to be here, for otherwise, even in this lonely place, he would not occupy the cabin. He was probably a hired gamekeeper, poaching on the side. He would not want Traver here, and he would not want the sheriff nosing around the island, either. He would want to take care of Traver by himself.

The man had come in and out of the cabin. He had the rifle in his hands, checking the action. His movements were calm and purposeful, and he gave Traver a good look at his face. It was a gaunt face, creased and hard, under heavy eyebrows, a shrewd face, curiously empty of emotion. Traver recognized that face, he had seen it all his life, throughout the South.

Ol Redneck kill me, do he get the chance. And he mean to get the chance.

The man went off in the direction of Snake-house, moving swiftly into the trees.

For the moment, considering his situation, Traver stayed right where he was. He watched the shrimp boat disappear along the delta. His mouth was dry, and he licked dew from the grass. Though the early sun had begun to warm him, he felt tired and stiff and very hungry, and this hunger encouraged him to loot the cabin.

Unreal in the morning mist, the trees were still. The Spanish moss hung everywhere, like silence. The man would go to Snake-house, to the landing, to pick up Traver's trail, but it would not lead him far. Traver had stayed clear of the sand path, moving wherever possible on the needle ground beneath the pines. Still, if he meant to loot the cabin, he should hurry. And he was half-risen when a huge blue heron, sailing above the cedars into which the hunter had disappeared, flared off with a squawk and thrash of heavy wings.

Traver sank to his knees again, heart pounding.

That was close to bein you last worldly move. I mean, he layin fo you, man, and he like to cotched you. I mean, he *smart*, doan you forget it, nigger. He know what you doin even fore you does it.

62

Traver waited again. When his heart stopped pounding, he began to laugh, a long quiet laugh that shook his big body like crying, and caused him to press his mouth to the crook of his arm. And he was surprised when tears came to his eyes, and the laughter became sobbing. He was frightened, he knew, and at the same time, he was unbearably excited.

You just a big black mule, you just a fool and a mule and a alligator all wrap into one.

He went on laughing, knowing his delight was dangerous, and all the more elated because of that. And as he laughed, he hummed to himself, in hunger.

In a while, far over toward the swamp, he heard the quack of startled black ducks, rising. When he saw their high circle over the trees, he got up on his haunches.

Could be dat a duck hawk, but most likely dat him. He over dar by Snake-house.

A string of ibis, drifting peacefully down the length of woods like bright white sheets of tissue, reassured him. Traver ran. In the open, he tensed for the rifle crack he could never have heard had it come, and zigzagged for the door. In less than a minute, he was back. He had a loaf of bread and matches, and was grinning wildly with excitement.

But now a fresh fear seized him. The hunter might return at any time, from any angle. If he did not hurry, he would no longer be able to maneuver without the terror of being seen. Traver stopped chewing, the stale bread dry in his mouth. Then he cut into the woods, loping in a low, bounding squat in the direction taken by the white man. At Graveyard-over-the-Bank, where once the cattle had been driven, penned, and slaughtered, he hid again. This place, a narrowing of the island, the man would sooner or later have to pass.

Traver stalked him all that day. Toward noon, the hunter went back to the cabin. Traver could hear him rummage for the bread, and he wondered if, in taking it, he might only have endangered himself further by becoming, in the white man's eyes, more troublesome. The man came out again and sat on the doorsill, eating. His face, still calm, was tighter, meaner, Traver thought. The rifle lay across his knees. Then he rose and went away into the woods, heading south-west toward Cottonmouth Dike, and Traver followed.

The man made frequent forays from the path, but he seemed to know that he would not surprise his quarry, that Traver was in all probability behind him, for though he moved stealthily out of habit, he made no real effort to conceal himself. Clearly, his plan was to lure Traver into a poor position, a narrow neck or sparsely wooded place where he might hope to turn and hunt him down. He set a series of ambushes, and now and then wheeled and doubled back along his trail. He was skillful and very quick, quick enough to frighten Traver, who several times was nearly trapped. Traver hung farther and farther behind, using his knowledge of the island to guess where the hunter would come and go, and never remaining directly behind, but quartering.

He was most afraid of the animals and birds which, hunting and hunted, could betray his whereabouts at any time.

The white man was tireless, and this intensity frightened Traver, too. He seemed prepared to stalk forever, carrying his provisions in his pocket. When he ate, he did it in the open, pointedly, knowing that Traver could never relax enough to hunt, could only watch and starve. By noon of the second day, Traver was desperate. When the man went west again, way over past Pig Root and Eagles Grave, Traver fled eastward to the landing and gorged on the coon oysters. Sated, he realized his mistake. He had a hundred yards of marsh to cross, back to the trees, and for all he knew, the hunter had doubled back again, and had a bead on him. He had done just what the man was waiting for him to do, he had lost the scent, and now any move he made might be the wrong one. He groaned at the thought of the vanished skiff—if only he'd gotten it ashore, and hidden it in the salt grass farther down. But now he was trapped, not only at the landing but on the island.

A bittern broke camouflage with a strangled squawk, causing Traver to spin around. In panic, he clambered up over the river bank and ran back to the trees. The woods were silent. There came a faint cry of snow geese over the delta, and the sharp rattle of a kingfisher back in the slough. Downwind, wild cattle caught his scent, retreating noisily. Or was that the coming of the hunter? He pressed himself to the black earth, in aimless prayer. The silence grew, cut only by the wash of river wind in the old-field pine. Then a wren called, Peter, Peter, Peter, and a hawk flicked quickly overhead in its direction.

Peter, Peter, Peet—

At dark, he fled into the marsh, and tried to rest in the reeds beneath a dike. Under the moon, much later, a raccoon picked its way along the bank, and he stunned it with his rabbit club. The coon played possum. When he crawled up to it, it whirled and bit him on the ankle. He struck it sharply with the stone end of the club, and it dragged itself into the reeds. He could not see it very well and, in a near frenzy of suppressed fear, he beat the dark shape savagely, long after it was dead. Panting, he sat and stared at the wet, matted mound of fur, the sharp teeth in the open, twisted mouth. He dared not light a fire with his stolen matches, and his gut was much too nervous to accept it raw. He left it where it lay and crept back to the woods and, in an agony of stealth, to Back-of-Ocean. He was overjoyed by the lamp in the cabin window.

He finally tuckered out, Traver told himself. The man done give old Traver up. Traver too spry for him.

The idea restored his confidence a little, and he chuckled without heart. He was still hungry, and he had no idea what his next move should be. Remembering the white man's face, he did not really believe he had given up the hunt, and this instinct was confirmed, at daybreak. The boat appeared again, and the white man met it, but he did not come out of the cabin. He stepped into the clearing from the yaupon on the other side. Traver had almost approached that way the night before. The light in the window had only been another trap.

Traver fought a wild desire to bolt. But he controlled himself, squeezing great fistfuls of earth between his fingers. He watched the hunter walk slowly to the beach and, resting his rifle butt on the silver roots of a hurricane tree, speak to the boatman. They were silent for a time, as if deciding something. Then the hunter shrugged, and shoved the boat from shore. It backed off with a grinding of worn gears. He returned to the cabin and came out of it a minute later. He had a cooked bone, and he pulled long strings of dry meat from it with his teeth. Traver stared at the lean yellow-brown of his face, the wrinkled neck, the faded khaki clothes and high, cracked boots against the soft greens of the trees and the red cassina berries. He stared at the bone. The man tossed it out in front of him, then tramped it into the ground and lit a cigarette. Breathing smoke, he leaned against the cabin logs and gazed around the clearing. Traver caught the cigarette scent on the air, and stirred uncomfortably. The man flipped the butt into the air, and together they watched it burn away upon the ground. Then he shouldered the rifle and went back to the woods, and once more Traver followed.

Who huntin who heah? Traver tried to smile. Who huntin who?

The fear was deep in him now, like cold. He started at every snap and crackle and cry of bird, sniffing the air for scents which could tell him nothing. There was only the stench of rotting vegetation, and the rank sweat of his fear. He crept along closer and closer to the ground, terrified lest he lose contact with the hunter. In his heart, he knew there was but one course open to him. He could not leave the island, and he could not be killed.

Both prospects were unimaginable. But he could kill.

Man, you in de swamp now. It you or him, dass all.

But he could not make himself accept this. He supposed he could kill a black man if he had to, and a white man could kill *him*. But a black man did not kill a white man unless the black man was insane.

Man, it doan matter what de color is, it just doan matter now. You in de swamp, and de swamp a different world. Dey ain't nobody left in dis heah world but you and him, and he figger dass too crowded. When ol Lo'd passed out de mens's hearts, dis heah man hid behind de do'. A man like dis heah man, you let him run where he de law, and he kill you if you black or white or blue. He ain't no more civilized den a cat gone wild. He doan hate you and he doan feel sorry, no more'n de cat do. You just a varmint dat got in de way, dass all.

But Traver doubted his own sense. Perhaps this man had nothing to hide, perhaps he was hunting legally, perhaps he would do no more than remove Traver from the island, or arrest him—how could he know that this man, given the chance, would shoot him down?

And yet he knew, as wild animals know, by instinct. He could smell it. He doubted his instinct because, himself civilized, he hated what it told him, because he wanted to believe that this man also was afraid, that a man would not shoot another down without first calling out to him to surrender.

Man, he ain't called, and he know you heah. He quiet as de grave. And you take it in you haid to call you'self, you fixin to get a bullet fo you answer.

Again that morning, he was nearly ambushed. This time a rabbit gave the man away. For the first time, Traver lost his nerve entirely. He ran back east along the island and stole out on the marsh, crawling along the dike bank where he had killed the coon, persuading his pounding heart that food was his reason for coming. But he knew before he got there that the raccoon would be gone. Black vultures and an eagle rose in silence from the bank, and there was a flat track in the reeds where an alligator had come and gone, and there were blue crabs clinging upside down to the grass at the edge of the ditch. In the marsh, the weak and dead have a brief existence.

Traver was shifting his position when a bullet slapped into the mudbank by his head. Its whine he heard afterward, a swelling in his ears as he rolled into the water and clawed at the brittle stalks of cane across the ditch. A wind of teal wings, rising out of Dead Oak Pond, blurred his racket in the brake. He crossed a reedy flat and slid into a small pool twenty yards away. The echo of the shot diminished on the marsh, and silence settled, like a cloud across the sun.

Then fiddler crabs snapped faintly on the flat. Where he had passed, their yellow claws protruded, open, from the holes.

But he knew the man would come, and he tried to control the choked rasp of his breath. And the man came, picking his lean way along the dike, stopping to listen, coming on, as Traver himself had often done, tracking crippled ducks for the plantation gunners. Against the bright, high autumn sky, the hunter's silhouette was huge.

Traver slipped the rabbit club from his belt.

The man had stopped just short of where Traver had lain. He squinted up and down the ditch. Though his face remained set, his right hand, wandering on the trigger guard and breech, betrayed his awareness that Traver might have a weapon.

He came a little farther, stopped again. He seemed on the point of calling out, but did not, as if afraid of intruding a human voice into this primeval silence. He bent and scratched his leg. Then, for a moment, scanning the far side of the dike, he turned his head.

Traver, straightening, tried to hurl the club, but it would not leave his hand. He ducked down and out of sight again. He told himself that the range had been too great, that the chance of a miss, however small, could not be taken. But he also knew he was desperate enough to have thrown it anyway, in agony, simply to bring an end to this suspense.

There was something else.

The man descended from the dike, on the far side. Almost immediately, he sank up to his knees, for there came a heavy, sucking sound as his boots pulled back. The man seemed to know that here, in the black resilience of the marsh, his quarry had him at a disadvantage, for he climbed back up onto the dike and took out a cigarette. This time, Traver thought he must call out, but he did not. Instead, he made his way back toward the woods.

Traver cursed him, close to tears. The hunter had only to watch from the trees at the end of the dike. Until dark, Traver was trapped. The hunter would sit down on a log and eat his food, while Traver lay in the cold pool and starved. The whole world was eating, hunting and eating and hunting again, in an endless cycle, while he starved. From where he lay, he could see a marsh hawk quartering wet meadows, and an eagle's patient silhouette in a dead tree. Swaying grass betrayed a prowling otter, and on a mud flat near him, two jack snipe probed for worms. Soon, in that stretch of ditch that he could see, a young alligator surfaced.

Thank de Lo'd it you what stole my coon. Thank de Lo'd dis pool too shaller fo you daddy.

The alligator floated, facing him. Only its snout and eyes disturbed the surface, like tips of a submerged branch.

What you waitin on, Ugly? You waitin on ol Traver, man, you got to get in line.

The insects had found Traver, and he smeared black mud on his face and hands. Northeast, a vulture circled slowly down on something else.

Whole world waitin on poor Traver. Whole world hangin round to eat on Traver.

And though he said this to cheer himself, and even chuckled, the sense of the surrounding marsh weighed down on him, the solitude. Inert, half-buried, Traver mourned a blues.

Black river bottom, black river bottom
Nigger sinkin down to dat black river bottom
Ain't comin home no mo'

Ol Devil layin at dat black river bottom
Black river bottom, black river bottom,
Waitin fo' de nigger man los' on de river
Dat ain't comin home no mo' . . .

At dark, inch by inch, circuitously, Traver came ashore. He knew now he must track the man and kill him. His nerves would not tolerate another day of fear, and he took courage from the recklessness of desperation.

Again the cabin was lit up, but this time he smelled coffee. The man's shadow moved against the window, and the light died out. The man would be sitting in the dark, rifle pointed at the open door.

The hunt ended early the next morning.

Traver bellied across a clearing and slid down a steep bank which here joined the high ground to the marsh. His feet were planted in the water at the end of Red Gate Ditch, and on his right was a muddy, rooted grove of yaupon known as Hog Crawl. The hunter was some distance to the eastward.

Traver had a length of dry, dead branch. He broke it sharply on his knee. The snap rang through the morning trees, and a hog grunted from somewhere in the Crawl. Then Traver waited, peering through the grass. He had his knife out, and his rabbit club. Lifting one foot from the water of the ditch, he kicked a foothold in the bank. Below him, the scum of algae closed its broken surface, leaving no trace of where the foot had been.

The man was coming. Traver could feel him, somewhere behind the black trunks of the trees. The final sun, which filtered through the woods from the ocean side, formed a strange red haze in the shrouds of Spanish moss. Out of this the man appeared. One moment there was nothing and the next he was there, startling the eye like a copperhead camouflaged in fallen leaves. He moved toward Traver until he reached the middle of the clearing, just out of Traver's range, facing the Hog Crawl. There he stood stiff as a deer and listened.

Traver listened too, absorbing every detail of the scene through every sense. The cardinal song had never seemed so liquid, the foliage so green, the smell of the earth so strong. Though tense to the breaking point, he felt powerfully alive, the trap was his, he was the hunter now, on his own ground.

And the white man shifted, stepping a little closer. The hog snuffled again, back in the yaupon. Traver could just make it out beneath the branches, a brown-and-yellow brindle sow, caked with dry mud. Now it came forward, curious. It would see Traver before it saw the white man, and it would give him away.

Traver swallowed. The sow came toward him, red-eyed. The white man, immobile, waited for it, also. When the sow saw Traver, it stopped, then backed away a little, then grunted and trotted off.

Traver flicked his gaze back to the man.

He was suspicious. Black eyes wide, head up, he froze. Then slowly the rifle swung around until it was pointed a few feet to Traver's left.

He gwine kill me now. Even do I pray, O Lo'd, he gwine kill me now.

Traver was backing down the bank as the man moved forward. Beneath the turned-down brim, the eyes were fixed on the spot to Traver's left. Traver flipped the butt of broken branch in the same direction. When the white man whirled upon the sound, Traver reared and hurled his club. He did not miss. It struck just as the shot went off.

Traver had rolled aside instinctively, but this same instinct drove him to his feet again and forward. The man lay still beside the rifle. The hand which had been groping for it fell back as Traver sprang. He pressed his knife blade to the white, unsunburned patch of throat beneath the grizzled chin.

Kill him, kill him now.

But he did not. Gasping, he stared down at the face a foot from his. It was bleeding badly from the temple but was otherwise unchanged. Pinning the man's arms with his knees, he pushed the eyelids open with his free hand. The eyes regarded him, unblinking, like the eyes of a wounded hawk.

"Wa'nt quite slick enough fo Traver, was you!" Traver panted. He roared hysterically in his relief, his laughter booming in the quiet grove. "You fall fo de oldes trick dey is, dass how smart you is, white folks!" He roared again into the silence. "Ol Traver toss de branch, ol white boy fooled, ol white boy cotch it in de haid! I mean! De oldes trick dey is!"

Traver glared down at him, hoarse, triumphant. The man lay silent.

Traver ran the knife blade back and forth across the throat, leaving a thin red line. He forced his anger, disturbed at how swiftly his relief replaced it.

"You de one dat's scairt now, ain't you? Try to kill dis nigger what never done you harm! You doan know who you foolin with, white trash, you foolin with a man what's mule and gator all wrap into one! And he gwine kill you, what you think 'bout dat?"

The man watched him.

"Ain't you nothin to say fore I kills you? You gwine pray? Or is I done killed you already?" Uneasy astride the body of the white man, Traver rose to a squat and pricked him with his knife tip. "Doan you play possum with me, now! You ain't foolin me no mo, I gwine kill you, man, you heah me?"

For the first time, Traver heard his own voice in the silence, and it startled him. He glanced around. The sun was bright red over the live oak trees, but quiet hung across the marsh like mist. Out of the corner of his eye, he watched the white man with suspicion, but the other did not stir.

He dead, Traver thought, alarmed. I done killed him dead.

Avoiding the unblinking eyes, he picked up the rifle and stared at it, then he laid it like a burial fetish back into the grass. Now he stepped back, knife in hand, and prodded the body with his toe.

"Git up, now!" he cried, startling himself again. "You ain't bad hurt, Cap'n, you just kinda dizzy, dass all. Us'ns is got to do some talkin, heah me now?"

But the body was still. A trail of saliva dribbled from the narrow mouth, and a fly lit on the grass near the bloody temple. Traver bent and crossed the arms upon the narrow chest.

"You fall fo de oldes trick in de world," Traver mourned, and shook his head. "Dass what you done." Badly frightened, he talked to comfort himself, glancing furtively around the clearing.

He started to back away, then bolted.

The man rolled over and up onto his knees, the rifle snatched toward his shoulder. He sighted without haste and fired. Then he reached for his hat and put it on, and turned the brim down all around.

Then he got up.

Traver was a powerful man and did not fall. He could still hear the echo and the clamor in the marsh, and he could not accept what was happening to him. He had never really believed it possible, and he did not believe it now. He dropped the knife and staggered, frowning, as the man walked toward him. The second bullet knocked him over backwards, down the bank, and when he came to rest, his head lay under water.

His instinct told him to wriggle a little further, to crawl away into the reeds. He could not move. He died.

Harper's Magazine
1957
An O'Henry Prize winner

A REPLACEMENT

Toward the end of the war, a certain Headquarters retreated across the Rhine, leaving behind one officer and a garrison of local conscripts. The officer had asked to be left, yet could give no reason; it was said that he was ill, and there was no time to investigate the matter.

The officer sat alone in his office, as if he had fallen asleep while directing its evacuation; a desk and two chairs were left him, and a clean rectangle on the floor where the filing cabinet had been.

Before the desk stood a prisoner and a guard.

In the new quiet, it seemed to the officer that, one way or another, the war was over for him, he had nothing to do with it anymore. He was tired, and full of doubt about his health. He was not surprised, therefore, that this prisoner looked precisely like himself, although younger and more frightened than he could ever remember having been.

The night guard, who stood behind this boy as if he had captured him single-handed, reported that the prisoner had come in out of the cold of his own accord, that he spoke German, and that his arm was broken. Also, that he was an enemy pilot.

The officer struggled with these facts, but they did not interest him nearly so much as the prisoner's appearance. Long ago, he thought, I saw that face in the mirror, but I was much younger than he is, I was only beginning.

He remained silent, absorbed with this thought.

The guard coughed loudly, and said,

"Herr Oberleutnant . . . "

Which made him laugh, yet the sound of his own laughter snapped his full attention to the two men before him. He wondered at the same instant how long they had been there, and why he felt so desperately like laughing.

"You speak German, then," the officer said, controlling himself. He studied the boy from under the visor of his cap, which was balanced between the top of the chair and his forehead. The chair itself was shoved away from the desk, permitting him to stretch a rigid full length, with the soles of his boots against the desk legs.

"My people come from Germany."

"Interesting," the officer said, folding his hands across his stomach. He reclined in silence.

The guard took advantage of the pause by tiptoeing backward and seating himself stealthily on a second chair by the door.

"Your first time in Germany?" the officer said, and laughed, not at his remark but at the conversational manner in which he had made it and at its reflection of his inability to concentrate.

The boy did not answer. His lifeless face announced that only routine questions could loosen his tongue.

Over the desk, the lighting wavered, ebbing like a sick man's breath, then strengthened again to sour the room with yellow. It trembled with the quaking walls against the night wind outside, casting its feeble rays upon the silence.

The officer watched the prisoner's eyes. He doesn't recognize our likeness, he thought, and he doesn't know what he's waiting for. On the other hand, neither do I, I don't understand, my own mind isn't doing my thinking for me at all, I am too full of queer ideas to work at the interrogation.

Although these thoughts were unnerving, they did not bother him as much as he knew they should, but only tired him further. His eyes were hidden from the prisoner by his visor, yet he could not close them. They had been open for more nights than he could remember, stretched and dry like bits of hide.

He thought, If I die, no German will have time to close them for me.

"You're very young," he said, startled by his own morbidity, and when the boy only waited, he said,

"Why do they send you now, so young, I mean? I thought we alone were down to our old men and puberts."

"I don't know," the boy said. He was standing at uncertain attention, one arm stiff against his side. "I'm a replacement."

"Really? Whom are you replacing?" the officer asked, fingering through his shirt the crucifix suspended from his neck, and thinking, *I wish he were replacing me.*

"A dead man," the boy said, staring at the officer.

How strange he should say that, the officer thought, whom can he mean?

"I'll have to question you," the officer sighed, "and send you away, but where's the sense in it, any more than letting you stand there?"

"I don't know," the boy muttered.

"You don't understand, you mean," the officer told him, and added, as if to the guard, "he doesn't understand."

"No, sir," the guard said, standing and sitting down again in confusion.

The officer looked from one to the other, twirling his cap on his finger.

"You've hurt your arm," he said to the prisoner.

"Yes."

"How?"

"When I hit the ground."

"This is part of your story?"

"Yes."

"Start from the beginning, then." The officer sat up suddenly, pleased with such efficiency, and banged his chair upon the floor.

"My plane was hit on a bomber escort mission, and when I jumped, my chute ignited and burned out in mid-air. I fell through a tree-top and broke my arm on the ground."

The boy's voice was monotone, as if he did not expect his story to be believed; he winced at the roar of the guard.

The officer raised his eyebrows, and the guard stood up, abashed.

"That's your story?"

"Yes."

"Our German ground is very hard," the officer said. He placed his cap on the desk. "I can quite believe that you broke your arm."

The guard laughed loudly again, reseating himself with a philosophical shake of his head.

"Guard," the officer said.

The guard vaulted from the chair and hastened forward.

"Bring me the interrogation file, Guard."

"But the files are gone, Herr Oberleutnant!"

"True." The officer paused. "Bring that chair for the prisoner, then."

He noticed in the eyes of the prisoner that the order had been taken as a punishment for the guard's rudeness, rather than as a consideration of himself; he noticed this, but it did not interest him. "You can wait outside," he added.

The boy sat down on the edge of the chair.

"Listen . . ." the officer started.

"It was the only tree in the field," the boy said. His voice was still monotone, but his eyes were wide. "I can't believe it myself."

"Listen," the officer said. "You won't understand this, but my mind has been playing tricks on me all night. You can't imagine what such a tale does to me. And besides, it's very late at night, which is all right, it's my duty to question you. However, I'm overtired, I'd expected a replacement, and nobody came. Now start all over again."

"I've told you the truth," the boy said.

"You fell out of a plane and hurt your arm, is that it?" the officer snapped. When the boy only coughed miserably, clutching the arm, he added more gently,

"You're frightened. Perhaps you will be more frightened when I tell you that, with a story like that one, you will have to be shot as a spy."

"But I'm not a spy," the boy said, moaning a little.

"Why did you give yourself up?"

"What would *you* have done?"

"That's beside the point. What would you have done if you hadn't hurt yourself, falling out of your plane?"

"I don't know. Probably the same."

"You've made a mistake," the officer said, putting his cap on again. "You could have escaped. Or hidden. Your chances would have been excellent, speaking German as you do. If I'd been you, I wouldn't have thought twice about it."

"I don't know *why* I came," the boy said. "I just came. I couldn't help myself."

"I can't understand such cowardice in you," the officer said, angry in spite of himself.

The prisoner said nothing.

"Did you expect me to believe such a tale?" the officer said. He tried to fire his questions briskly, to show that no nonsense would be tolerated, but he could not, he was too tired to frighten anybody. Anyway, the boy was clearly frightened already. And there was something alluring about his story, too, that detail about the only tree in the field, for instance. He sensed that if he were the other, he would never tell such a story unless he expected to be believed.

"Yes," the boy was saying, "I came because I expected to be

believed."

So. And yet the story was impossible. The officer felt uneasy at not having dismissed it out of hand.

"No," he said at last, "You came here because you were frightened."

"Yes," the boy said. "I was frightened at having been allowed to live."

"Of course," the officer said, then added hastily, "I mean to say, there is nothing in international law that prevents the execution of a spy just because he is a coward."

"But I'm not a spy," the boy said.

"Nor a coward," the officer agreed, smiling.

"I don't know," the boy said. "I don't think so."

"Of course not," the officer said. He stretched back again in his chair and studied the ceiling. The empty office tired him, as if his responsibility had been removed with the filing cabinet, taking with it his brain and spine, all the components of himself which gave him the energy to live. At this moment, his life seemed as unreal as the war which, like a thinning mist, lost its stature as it overtook them.

"Tell me," he said, "What would you do, in my position?"

"I don't know," the boy said. He seemed absorbed by the pain in his arm.

"I only ask you because I think we are in many ways alike," the officer grumbled, and lapsed into silence.

"About me, you mean?" the boy said.

"About anything at all," the officer said, and after a moment, "But just now, about you."

"I don't know," the boy said.

"You'd do well to get an idea," said the officer angrily.

"Why not go and see for yourself," the prisoner complained, rocking back and forth over his arm. "There are bits of the parachute still in the tree."

"I thought it burned up in mid-air."

"It did. I wish you'd believe me."

"I *do* believe you," the officer told him, and they exchanged a look of surprise. "But who's going to believe *me?*"

"Come and see, then. Bring the guard."

"And besides," the officer said, "even if I do believe you, it's still impossible. How far is it?"

"Maybe three kilometers."

"That's too far. My faith would never get me there."

"Can't we take an auto?" the prisoner said.

The officer waived an arm at the empty room.

"They took that, too. I can't be expected to walk."

"If you don't," the boy said, "I'll be shot as a spy."

"What in hell did you expect," the officer shouted, "sneaking in here like this!" He shifted violently in his chair, turning sideways to the prisoner. "That's true, though," he conceded, and shifted back again.

"What were you bombing tonight, may I ask?"

"An artillery emplacement, at the far end of the valley."

"That was moved a week ago," the officer told him. "Your people have made a mistake."

"I don't know," the boy said. "I never got there."

"Take my word for it, then," the officer said, "I'm taking yours for much more."

"As a matter of fact, " he added, drawing his chair to the desk, "you've got no business here at all. The whole night's a mistake from start to finish, you've been saved for nothing, because you ran here spouting German and saying you fell out of a plane that was bombing an artillery emplacement that wasn't even there. You'll be shot for your pains."

"You don't believe me, then?" the boy said. His face was surly with fear.

"Another man would shoot you for a spy," the officer said. He rose abruptly from the desk and stalked around it, circling several times between the prisoner and its front, then going around the prisoner to stare at him from behind.

"You won't change your story?" he suggested. "Say simply that you buried your parachute and fell into our hands by mistake?"

"All right, if that will help any," the boy said. "But it's not the truth."

"No," the officer said, "but it sounds like it, at least."

He strode up and down the barren room with his hands on his hips, studying the back of the other's head as he passed.

"You want to go to prison camp, then?"

"I'd like to see a doctor," the boy muttered, turning his head around.

The officer stopped short.

"I'm sorry," he said. "I don't mean to play with you. It's just that I'm tired, I feel like laughing hysterically, and I can't make up my mind to do anything about you, or do anything about myself, for that matter."

Please," the boy said. "Come and see."

"All right," the officer said, and they exchanged another look of surprise. "It's a question of life and death, I suppose."

But the boy only waited, not understanding.

The officer laughed aloud at a deep impulse to cry, dragging on his greatcoat and shouting furiously for the guard.

Outside, the North wind clasped them in a grip of cold, howling and buffeting over the land, and the night clouds flew beneath the moon, which glazed the winter patches by the roadside and the trees wet black with March. The officer was excited by the night, and tried to sing out his exhilaration to the others—"Look at me!" he wanted to cry, "can you see something happening?"— but it sounded somehow foolish to him, he did not understand it himself, and only said to the guard,

"I am sorry to make you walk so far, since it has nothing to do with you."

But the guard did not seem to hear him, and the boy repeated it for him in a voice exactly like his own, so much so that the guard answered the officer instead, as if the prisoner had not spoken.

"How alike our voices are!" cried the officer, but the words crumbled against the wind and passed unheard.

Doomsday night, he thought, and wondered why. Because nothing matters any more, it is the end of the world for me, he decided, alarmed because it didn't matter to him. Still, the thought was frightening; he squeezed the arm of the prisoner to be sure he had not vanished.

"We'll be able to see the remains of the parachute and everything?" he demanded, as if otherwise he would only be cheated at the last moment.

"Yes," the boy said. His chattering teeth destroyed the word, but his nod reassured the officer, who marched him down the road more quickly than ever.

A little further, the officer shouted,

"I realize this is all impossible, you are tricking me in some way, yet you must not believe I am so simple as I may appear. It is simply that you have a pleasant face, you remind me of my boyhood, and I would be very sorry to have you shot without first ascertaining the facts of the matter!"

But the boy only mumbled inaudibly within his upturned collar.

They hurried faster, turning from the road and mounting the frozen valleyside to the highest field. Alone on the ridge, a great tree ruled the winter sky.

The guard was finished by the pace and sat down immediately, with scarcely the strength to peer upwards into the branches, but the officer walked forward slowly, his heart alive with the exertion.

"It's just as you say," he breathed. The wind had fallen, leaving his whisper to wander in the stillness.

He stooped to pick up the discarded harness belt but only held it in both hands, as gently as a holy relic, without looking at it. His eyes were fastened on the strips of blackened silk, which trailed from the branches above like devil's ornaments. The branches were twisted and broken, and a remnant of snow at the ancient roots was scarred with fallen twigs.

A miracle, he thought, I have seen a *miracle,* or I am going insane. He whirled and stared at the boy, who moved towards him with hesitation.

"I believed you. Forgive me for doubting myself."

The boy nodded, waiting, and the guard stood up, glancing from one to the other.

"You were saved," the officer said, "and then you were sent to me. Why?"

But the boy was staring at the tree, awed anew by the scene of his fall.

"There's nothing to be afraid of," the officer told him. "Tomorrow a train of exchange prisoners passes through for Switzerland. You will go with them."

They glanced at the guard who, following the words of the officer with his lips, still grunted in amazement.

"How can you do that?" the boy said.

"I can hardly send a man who has won a new life to prison camp," the officer said. He felt a little dizzy.

"But surely you'll get in trouble."

"With whom?" the officer whispered.

"No," he added, more loudly, "it is too late to get in trouble. Everything will be over soon, and it doesn't matter."

"Thank you," the boy said. He came forward and shook the officer's hand. "Thank you very much."

"You have a new life," the officer said, embracing him. "Make a good job of it."

The boy pulled away, embarrassed.

"Thank you," he repeated.

Their brief contact had filled the older man with peace; his eyes relaxed, then closed. He tried to open them but could not, yet it seemed to him he could distinguish the silhouette of the guard.

"Guard," he said, "you have witnessed everything?"

"Yes, Herr Oberleutnant," said the voice of the guard.

"It is a miracle, Guard."

"Yes, Herr Oberleutnant."

"Take this man to the doctor's house immediately. He will go on that train tomorrow," the officer said. He felt his way backward to the tree and sat down, resting his head against the trunk. So, he thought. It is over now.

The guard's voice came faintly; the wind was rising again. The boy called to him, " . . . coming with us, then?"

"God be with you," the officer said, but the wind scattered the words and sealed his lungs with cold.

Paris Review
1952

THE WOLVES OF AGUILA

On those rare occasions when a lean gray wolf wandered north across the border from the Espuela Mountains, trotting swiftly and purposefully into the Animas Valley or the Chiricahuas or Red Rock Canyon as so many had in years gone by, describing a half-circle seventy miles or more back into Mexico, and leaving somewhere along its run a mangled sheep or a mutilated heifer, then Miller was sent for and Miller would go. He was a wolf hunter, hiring himself out on contract to ranchers and government agencies, and if the killing for which he was paid was confined more and more to coyotes and bobcats, the purpose of his life remained the wolf. He considered the lesser animals unworthy of his experience, deserving no better than the strychnine and the cyanide guns which filled the trunk of his sedan. Even the sedan had been forced upon him, when the wolf runs which once traced the border regions of New Mexico and Arizona had become so few and faded as to no longer justify the maintenance of a saddle pony. The southerly withdrawal of the gray wolf into the brown, dust-misted mountains of Chihuahua and Sonora had come to Will Miller as a loss, a reaction he had never anticipated. In his heart, he felt further persecution of the wolf unjustified, and was uneasily aware that each random kill he now effected contributed to the death of a wild place and a way of life which he knew was all he had.

Nevertheless, with mixed feelings of elation and penitence, he would travel to the scene of the last raid. There, he would

81

scout the area for "scent posts" with fresh wolf sign and, kneeling on a piece of calf hide, work his clean, steel traps into the earth with ritualistic care, rearranging every stick and pebble when he had finished, and carrying off the displaced dirt on the hide. His hands were gloved and his soles were smeared with the dung of the livestock using the range, and leaving the scene, he moved away backward, scratching out his slightest print with a frayed stick. Nor did he visit his traps until he was certain that the wolf had had time to come again, gauging this according to the freshness of the sign and according to his instinct. Because of his silence and solitary habits—made more striking by a wind-eroded visage and the fierce tint of his Navajo blood—Miller was credited with the ability to think like an animal. His success was a border legend, and while it was true that he understood its creatures very well, he was successful because he did not take their timeless traits for granted. The dark history of *Canis lupus,* the great gray wolf of the world, he considered an important part of his practical education. Not that Miller accepted the old tales of werewolves and wolf-children, or not, at least, in the modern areas of his mind. But the heritage in him of the Old People, the deep-running responses to the natural signs and sacraments, did not discount them. The eerie intelligence of this night animal, its tirelessness and odd ability to vanish, had awed him more than once, and he had even imagined, in his long solitude, that should he ever pursue it into the brown haze to the south, the wolf spirit would revenge itself on that unfamiliar ground. Miller knew that such ideas were heathenish, but they lent his life a mystery and meaning that the church missions could not replace, and his mind asked no more. He was not a modern Indian, and he shunned the modern towns. Like the wolf itself, he abided by older laws.

The night forces of nature, to Will Miller, were incarnate in the Aguila wolf, which was known to have slaughtered sixty-five sheep in a single night and laid waste the stock in western Arizona for eight long years, fading back into the oblivion of time in 1924. One trapper in pursuit of it had disappeared without a trace, and Miller had always wondered if, at some point in that man's last terrible day beneath the sun, the Aguila wolf had not passed nearby, pausing in its ceaseless round to scent the dry, man-tainted air before padding on about its age-old business. Somewhere its progeny still hunted, and he often thought that the black male which once circled his traps for thirteen months and dragged the one which finally caught it forty miles must have descended from the old Aguila.

Ordinarily, he had little trouble. Within a week or ten days of its raid, the usual wolf would trot north out of Mexico again, and retracing its hunting route in a counter-clockwise direction, investigate the scent posts, pausing at each to void itself and scratch the earth. At one of these, sooner or later, it would place its paw in a slight depression, the dirt would give way, and the steel jaws would snap on its foreleg. If its own bone was too heavy to gnaw through, and the trap well staked, it would finally lie down and wait. It would sense Miller's coming and, if still strong enough, would stand. Though its hair would bristle, it rarely snarled. Invariably, Miller stood respectfully at a distance, as if trying to see in the animal's flat gaze the secret of his own fascination. Then he would dispatch it carefully with a .38 revolver. But when the wolf lay inert at his feet, a hush seemed to fall in the mesquite and paloverde, as if the bright, early-morning desert had died with the shot. The red sun, rising up, would whiten, and the faint smell of desert flowers fade, and the cactus wrens would still. In the carcass, already shrunken, lay the death of this land as it once was, and in the vast silence a reproach. The last time, Miller had broken his trap, and sworn that he would never kill a wolf again.

Some years passed before two animals, hunting together according to the reports, made kills all along the border, from Hidalgo County in New Mexico to Cochise and Santa Cruz Counties in Arizona, with scattered raids as far west as Sonoita, in Sonora. They used the ancient runs and developed new ones, but their wide range and unpredictable behavior had defeated all efforts at trapping them. The ranchers complained to the federal agencies, which in turn sent for Will Miller.

Miller at first refused to go. But he had read of the two wolves, and his restlessness overcame him. A few days later, he turned up in the regional Wildlife Office, a small, dark, well-made man of forty-eight in sweated khakis, with a green neckerchief and worn boots and a battered black felt hat held in both hands. Beneath a lank hood of ebony hair, his hawk face, hard and creased, was pleasant, and his step and manner quiet, unobtrusive. He had all his possessions with him. These included eight hundred dollars, a change of clothes, and the equipment of his profession in the sedan outside, as well as an indifferent education, a war medal, and the knowledge that, until this moment, he had never done anything in his simple life that had dishonored him. Placing his hat on the game agent's desk, he picked restlessly through the reports. Then he asked questions. Angry with himself for being there, he hardly listened while the agent explained that the two wolves seemed immune to ordinary methods, which was why Will Miller had been sent for. Miller ignored the first name and the compliment. Unsmiling, he asked if the two wolves were really so destructive that they couldn't be left alone. The agent answered that Miller sounded scared of *Canis lupus* after all these years and, because Miller's expression made him uneasy, laughed too loudly.

"Them wolves was here before we come," Miller said. "I'd like to know they was a few left when we go."

Miller went west to Ajo, where he got drunk and visited a woman and, before the evening was out, got drunk all over again. He was not an habitual drinker, and drank heavily only in the rueful certainty that he would be sick for days to come. Later he drove out into the desert and staggered among the huge shapes of the saguaros, shouting.

"I'm comin after you, goddam you, I'm comin, you hear that? Will Miller, Miller, Miller!"

And he shook his fist toward the distant mountains of Mexico. In doing so, he lost his balance and sat down hard, cutting his outstretched hand on a leaf of yucca. Glaring at the blood, black in the moonlight, he began to laugh. "Miller, Miller, Miller," he mimicked himself softly, after a time. But a little later, awed and sobered by the hostile silhouettes of the desert night, he licked at the black patterns traced upon his hand and shivered. Then he lay down flat upon his back and stared at the eternity of stars.

Toward dawn, closing his eyes at last, he sighed, and wondered if it could really be that he felt like crying. He jeered at himself instead. Unable to admit to loneliness, he told himself it was time he settled down, had children. He could decide who and how and where first thing in the morning. But a few hours later, getting up, he felt too sick to consider the idea. He cursed himself briefly and sincerely, and headed south toward Sonoita, where the wolves had been last reported.

The town of Sonoita lies just across the border from the organpipe cactus country of southern Arizona, on the road to Puerto Peñasco and the Gulf of California. Miller arrived there at midmorning. The heat was awesome, even for this seared land, as menacing in its still might as more violent weather elsewhere, and the Mexican border guards were apathetic, waving him through from beneath the shelter of their shed. Miller had a headache from the alcohol and desert glare and, making inquiries in the town, found no one who understood him. Finally, by dint of repeating, *"Lobo, lobo,"* into the round, rapt faces, he was led ceremonially to the parched remains of a steer outside the town. The carcass had been scavenged by the people, and a moping vulture flopped clumsily into the air. The trail was cold. Since Sonoita lay on the edge of the Gran Desierto, he did not believe that the wolves would wander farther west. From here, he would have to work back east, to New Mexico, if necessary.

Yet the villagers picked insistently at his shoulder— *sst! Señor sst!"*—and pointed westward. When he stared at them, then shook his head and pointed east, they murmured humbly among themselves, but one old man again extended a bony, implacable arm toward the desert. Like children, mouths slack, hands diffident behind their backs, the rest surrounded Miller, their black eyes bright as those of reptiles. *Sí amigo. Sí, sí.* They gravitated closer, not quite touching. *Sí, sí.* Abruptly, he pushed through them and returned into the town.

Clutching a beer glass in the cantina, encircled by his silent following, he knew he had not made a thorough search for wolf sign, and could not do so in his present state of mind. The prospect of long days ahead in the dry canyons, piecing out the faded trail, oppressed him so that he sat stupefied. He felt sick and uneasy and, in some way he could not define, afraid. He wanted to talk to someone, to flee from his forebodings, and he thought of a nice woman he knew in Yuma. But Yuma lay westward a hundred miles or more, via an old road across the mountain deserts to San Luis and Mexicali. He did not know the road, and he had heard tales of the violence of this desert, and he dreaded the journey through an unfamiliar land in his present condition, and in such heat. On the other hand, these people had directed him toward the west. How could they know? Considering this, his palms grew damp, and he felt dizzy. Still, by way of San Luis, he could reach Yuma by mid-afternoon and come back, in better spirits, tomorrow morning. Meanwhile, the wolves might kill again in Sonoita, leaving fresh sign. And if he got drunk enough, he thought, he might even come back married.

"To hell with it," he told the nodding Mexicans. "I'll go."

Outside, the heat struck him full in the face, stopping him short. His lungs squeezed the dry air for sustenance, and his nose pinched tight on the fine mist of alkali shrouding the town. In the shade, the natives and their animals squatted mute, awaiting the distant rains of summer. The town was inert, silent, in its dull awareness of Miller's car.

At the garage, Miller checked his oil and water carefully, knowing he should carry spare water with him, for the San Luis Road, stretching away into the Gran Desierto, would be long and barren. But he could not locate a container of any kind, and his growing apprehension irritated him, and on impulse he left without the water, quitting the town in a swirl of dust and gravel. Once on the road, however, he felt quite foolish, and he was not out of sight of the last adobe hut when he caught himself glancing at the oil pressure and water temperature gauges. He did it again a few minutes later.

The road ran west through low, scorched hills before curving south into the open desert. At one point it ran north to Quitoba-quito Springs, the only green place on the San Luis Road. Miller stopped the car. Across the springs, beneath a cottonwood, he saw a hut; a family of Papagos, two dogs, and a wild-maned horse gazed at him, motionless. The dogs were silent. In the treetops, two black, shiny phainopeplas fluttered briefly and were still.

"How do," Miller called. The Indians observed him, unblinking. It occurred to Miller that his was the only voice in this dead land, where people answered him, when they answered at all, with nods and grunts and soft, indecipherable hisses. He stood a moment, unwilling to think, then returned slowly to the sedan.

For a mile or so beyond the springs, a gravel road detoured from a stretch of highway left long ago in half-repair. The detour was rutted and pocked with holes, and he could barely keep the toiling car in motion. He was easing it painfully onto the highway again when he heard a clear, animal cry. The sound was wild and shrill, and startled Miller, braking the sedan, he stalled it. In the taut silence, the cry was repeated, and a moment later he glimpsed a movement at the mouth of a hollow in a road bank. An animal the size of a large dog slipped from the hole. In the glare, he did not recognize it as a child until it stood and approached the car. This creature, a boy of indefinite age, was followed instantly by another, who paused on all fours at the cave entrance before joining the first. The latter stood already at the window, fixing Miller with clear, flat elliptical eyes located high and to the side of his narrow face. His brother—for their features were identical—had brown hair rather than black, and his eyes were dull, seeing everything and reflecting nothing. Over the other's shoulder, he looked past Miller rather than at him, and after a moment turned his head away, as if scenting the air. Then the first boy smiled, a humorless smile which traveled straight back along his jaw instead of curling, and pointed his finger toward the west. When he lowered his hand, he placed it on the door handle.

Miller could not make himself speak. He stared at the hole from which the two had crept, unable to believe they had really come out of it, unable to imagine what they were doing here at all. His first thought had been that these boys must belong to the

Papago family at the springs, but one look at their faces told him this could not be so. These heads were sharp and clear-featured, reminiscent of something he could not recall, with a certain hardness about the mouth and nostrils, and fine white teeth. There was none of the blunt impassivity of the Papagos. There was nothing of poverty about them, either, and yet clearly they were homeless, without belongings of any kind. Still, they might be bandit children. He peered once again into the black eyes at the window, but his efforts to remember where he had seen that gaze were unsuccessful, and he shook his head to clear his dizziness. The boys watched him without expression, and after a while, when he did nothing, the older one opened the door and slipped into the car, and the second followed.

Miller felt oddly under duress, and moving the car forward onto the highway, glanced uneasily at the gauges. It upset him that the Indians had not inquired as to where he was going. On the San Luis Road, one came and one went, but one made certain of a destination, and he had the feeling that, were he to go mad and drive his car off southward across the hard desert into oblivion, those two would accompany him with foreknowledge and without surprise.

At last he said, in his poor Spanish:

"En donde va? A San Luis? Mexicali?"

The older boy smiled his curious smile and nodded, hissing briefly between white teeth. Miller took this to mean, *"Sí."*

"San Luis?" Miller said.

The boy nodded.

"Mexicali?" Miller said, after a moment.

The boy nodded. Either he did not understand, or the matter was of no importance to him. He raised his hand in a grotesque salute and smiled again. The eyes of the other boy switched back and forth, observing their expressions.

Though the heat had grown, the day had darkened and odd clouds, wild scudding blots of gray, swept up across the sallow sky from the remote Gulf. A wind came, fitfully at first, fanning sand across the highway. Miller, in a sort of trance, clung to the wheel. His car, which he knew he was driving too fast, was straining in the heat, and he wondered at the intensity of his relief when a large orange truck, the first sign of life in miles of thinning mesquite and saguaro, came at him out of the bleached distances ahead. He glanced at the two boys. They seemed to have sensed the coming of the truck long before Miller himself, for their eyes were fixed upon it, and the eyebrows of the elder were raised, alert.

As the truck neared, an arm protruded from the cab and flagged Miller to a stop.

The truck driver, lighting a brown cigarette, peered about him at the hostile desert before speaking, as if sharing the desolation with Miller. He then asked in Spanish the distance to Sonoita. Miller, who was now counting every mile of the hundred-odd to San Luis, knew the exact distance, and suspected the truck driver knew it, too. The chance meeting on the highway was, for both of them, a respite, a source of nourishment for the journey which, like the springs at Quitobaquito, was not to be passed up lightly. However, he could not think of the correct Spanish numeral, and when the other repeated the question, inclining his head slightly to peer past Miller at the Indians, Miller turned to them for help. Both boys stared straight ahead through the windshield. The Mexican driver repeated the question in what Miller took to be an Indian dialect, but still the boys sat mute. The older maintained his tense, alert expression, as if on the point of sudden movement.

"Treinta-cinco," Miller said at last, choosing an approximate round figure.

The driver thanked him, glancing once again at the two boys. He exchanged a look with Miller, then shrugged, forcing his machine into gear as he did so. The truck moaned away down the empty road, and the outside world it represented became a fleeting speck of orange in the rear-view mirror. When Miller could see it no longer, and the solitude closed around him, he inspected his temperature gauge once again. The red needle, which had climbed while the car was idling, returned slowly to a position just over normal, flickered, and was still.

The road ran on among gravel ridges, which mounted endlessly and sloped away to nothing. Only stunted saguaros survived in this country, their ribs protruded with desiccation, and in an abandoned hawk's nest testified to the fact that life had somehow been sustained here. Miller, who had seen no sign of wildlife since leaving the springs, wondered why a swift creature like a hawk would linger in such a place when far less formidable terrains awaited it elsewhere. And of course it had not remained. The nest might be many years old, as Miller knew, and the hawk young, mummified, might still be in it. On this sere, stifled valley floor, a crude dwelling, forsaken and untended, would remain intact for decades, with only dry wind to eat at it, grain by grain. Not, he thought, that any man could survive here, or even the Mexican wolf. And he had convinced himself of this when, at a long bend in the road, an outcropping of rock he had seen from some miles away was transformed by the muted glare into a low building of adobe and gray wood.

Removing his foot from the accelerator, he wiped his forehead with the back of a cold hand. The black sedan, still in gear, whined down across a gravel flat of dead saguaros.

The cantina lay fetched up against a ridge just off the highway, as if uprooted elsewhere and set down again, like tumbleweed, by some ill wind. Around it the heat rose and fell in shimmers; he thought it abandoned until he saw the hot glitter of a trash heap to one side. There were no cars or horses. Beside him, the older boy stared straight ahead, but he gave Miller the feeling that his vision encompassed the cantina, on one side, and Miller himself on the other. Both boys were pressed so close to the far window that there was a space between them and Miller on the narrow seat, and a tension as tight as heat filled the small compartment. Miller opened his door abruptly and got out. When the two turned to watch him, he pointed at the cantina and waited. After a moment, the dark boy reached across the younger one to the door handle, and both slipped out on the far side.

By the doorway, Miller paused and touched a hide stretched inside out upon the wall, allowing the Indians to draw near him and trail him into the cantina. He could not put away his dread, and the idea of leaving them alone with the car and equipment made him uneasy. But although they had moved forward, the two boys paused when he paused, like stalking animals. Heads partly averted, squinting in the violent sun of noon, they followed his hand upon the pelt, as if his smallest move might have its meaning for them.

For a moment, indecisive, he inspected the sun-cracked skin, through the old wounds of which the grizzled hair protruded. The wolf had been nailed long ago against the wall, and although most of the nails had fallen away, it maintained its tortured shape on the parched wood. With the tar paper and tin, the hide now served to patch the shack's loose structure. One flank and shoulder shifted in the wind from the Gran Desierto, and the claws of the right forefoot, still intact, stirred restlessly, a small, insistent scratching which Miller stifled by bending the claws into the slats. In doing so, he freed a final nail, and the upper quarter of the hide sagged outward from the wall, revealing the scraggy fur. Miller stooped to retrieve the nail. Half-bent, he stopped, then straightened, glancing back at the mute boys. Their narrow eyes shone flat, unblinking. He turned and moved through the doorless opening, stumbling on the sill.

In a room kept dark against the glare, a man stood behind the bar. He stared blindly at the blank walls, as if permanently ready to do business but unwilling to solicit it. The only sound was a raw, discordant clanging of a loose, tin sheet upon the roof, the only movement dust in the bright doorway. For a moment, Miller imagined him dead, but at the tip of a brown cigarette stub in the center of his mouth was a small glow.

"Buenos dias," he said.

The proprietor's answer was a soft tentative whispering scarcely audible above the clanging of the tin. Asking for a beer, Miller whispered, too. In answer, the man reached behind him into a black vat of water, drawing out a bottle with no label. He held it at arm's length like a trophy, the stale water sliding down his wrist. The vat, roiled by his hand, gave off a fetid odor of decay.

"All right," said Miller. *"Sí."*

He turned to locate the two boys. The older one stood outside the doorway, but the other was not in sight. Miller waved at the first to enter, but the boy did not stir. The proprietor, glimpsing him for the first time, looked startled. Miller took the tepid beer and requested two bottles of soda. Surprised, the man held up two fingers.

"There's another outside," Miller explained. He awaited the warm bottles, then walked quickly to the door, and the boy gave way. The other was squatted beneath the pelt, staring away over the desert. Though his head did not move, his eye flickered once or twice, aware of Miller, who sensed that, should he make a sudden motion, this creature would spring sideways and away, coming to rest, still watching him, after a single bound. Wild as they were, however, the two seemed less afraid of him than intent upon him. He could not rid himself of the notion that these wild, strange boys had been awaiting him in their cave near the Quito-baquito Springs.

They're just boys, he told himself.

The dark boy picked his way closer and took the two bottles of soda from Miller's hands. The exchange was ceremonial, without communication. The squatting boy, in turn, received his bottle from the other, clutching it with both hands and sniffing it over before bending his head and sucking the liquid upward with the aid of his tongue.

Miller returned inside to get his beer, and leaned backward heavily against the counter. His headache had grown worse, and the smell of the water on his bottle sickened him. He put it down, seizing the counter as a wave of vertigo shrouded his sight, and the boy in the doorway wavered in black silhouette. From somewhere near at hand, a soft voice probed for his attention. He recovered himself, sweating unnaturally, heart pounding.

"Lobo, lobo . . . ."

"Yes," he heard his own voice say, "that's a fine wolf hide out there . . . ."

"*. . . el lobo de Aguila . . . .*"

"No," Miller murmured. *"No es posible."*

"Sí, sí," hissed the proprietor. *"Sí, sí."*

"No," Miller repeated. He made his way to a crate against the wall and sagged down upon it, clasping his damp hands in a violent effort to squeeze out thought.

"Sí, amigo. El lobo de Aguila . . . ."

Wind shook the hut, and spurts of sand scraped at the outside wall. Miller heard the crack of stiffened skin as the wolf hide fell. He pitched to his feet in time to see it skitter across the yard toward the open desert, in time to see the squatting boy run it down in one swift bound, leaving his feet at the last second and landing neatly on all fours. He crouched on it, eyeing Miller over his left shoulder, the hair on the back of his head erect in the hot wind. At Miller's approach, he backed away a little distance, not quite cringing. Miller took the hide to the proprietor, who peered at all of them out of the shadows. The dark boy, when Miller glanced at him, smiled his wide, sudden smile.

The water in his radiator was still boiling when he removed the cap. He refilled the radiator with liquid from the beer vat inside, aware of the tremor in his hand. Paying the man, he dropped the money to the ground and had to grope for it. The two boys moved toward the car in response to some signal between them, and the man in the doorway, clutching the hide, hissed for Miller's attention.

"Señor . . . ."

He did not continue, and would not meet Miller's eyes.

"Adios," Miller said, after a moment, and the man's lips moved, but the whisper perished in the wind.

The motor, still hot, was hard to start, and the car, once moving, handled sluggishly. Miller rolled the windows up to close out the gusts of heat, but after a moment he could not catch his breath. Gasping, he rolled them down again. The two boys watched him.

According to his reckoning they were now halfway to San Luis. In early afternoon, the temperature had risen and the glare, oddly bright beneath an intermittent sun, was painful to his eyes. He saw with difficulty. His passengers seemed not to mind the heat, absorbed as they were with his expressions, the movements of his hands. Miller's intuitions ran headlong through his mind, but a curious despair, a resignation, entered with them.

He would reach San Luis or he would not, and that was all.

The sedan was passing south of the Cabeza Prieta Mountains, great tumbled barrens looming up out of the foothills to the northward. Somewhere up there, Miller had heard, lay the still body of a flyer, who only last week had left a note in his grounded plane and wandered west in search of help. He had not been found. In this weather, in this desert, a man made a single mistake, a single, small mistake—say, a mislaid hat, a neglected landmark, an unfilled canteen . . . . He must have expressed part of this thought aloud, for the dark boy was nodding warily. When Miller squinted at him, he smiled.

"You wouldn't last six hours out there," Miller told him, "don't matter who you are. You'd die like dogs."

The boy nodded, smiling.

Miller laughed harshly, and the second boy sat forward on the edge of his seat, eyes wide. Abruptly, Miller stopped and turned away. He felt lightheaded, a little drunk.

The landscape altered quickly now, and mountains appeared in scattered formations to the south. Their color was burnt black rather than brown, and their outlines looked crusted. Farther on, they crowded toward the road, extending weird shapes in heaps of squat, black boulders. The dull gravel of the desert floor was invaded, then replaced by sand, and the last stunted saguaros disappeared. With every mile, the sand increased in volume, overflowing the rock and creeping up the dead crevasses. The huge boulders sank down, one by one, beneath bare dunes, until finally the distances were white, scarred here and there with outcroppings of darkness. On the road itself, broad tongues of sand seeped out from the south side, and the sky turned to a sick, whitish pall, like the smoke of subterranean fires.

They had entered the Gran Desierto. He thought of the mountains of the moon.

Miller looked a last time at his gauges. The oil pressure was stable still, but the temperature needle, a streak of bright red in the monotone of his vision, was climbing. He knew he should slow the whining car, but he could not. Huddled together, his passengers sat rigid, eyes narrowed to slits against the sea of white. The younger one, tongue out, was panting audibly.

Miller tried to laugh, but no sound came. The dark boy gazed at Miller, then placed his arm about his brother's shoulder.

A tire split before the water went, and the car swerved onto the sand shoulder of the road. He wrenched at the wheel in a spasm of shock, and the sedan lurched free again like a mired animal, stalling and coming to rest as the rear tire settled. Miller fought for breath. He sat a moment blinking, as the sand, in wind-whipped sheets, whitened the pavement. Then he got out, and the two boys followed. Retreating to a little distance, they observed him as he opened the trunk and yanked the jack and lug wrench and spare tire from the litter of bags and traps.

The cement was too hot to touch, and the unseen sun too high in the pale sky to afford shade. Miller spread his bedroll and kneeled on it, working feverishly but ineffectually. He felt near to fainting, and the blown sand seared his face, and he burned his hands over and over on the hot shell of the sedan. But he managed at last to free the tire, and was fighting the spare into place when a sound behind him made him whirl. The dark boy stood over him, holding the iron lug wrench.

Miller leapt up, stumbling backward.

"Christ!" his voice croaked. Crouching, he came forward again, stalking the child, who dropped the wrench and moved away. Miller picked it up and followed him. The younger was squatting on the roadside, lifting one scorched foot and then the other, and emitting a queer, mournful whine. His brother took his hand and pulled him away. Unwilling to leave the shelter of the car, they kept just out of reach. When Miller stopped, they stopped, also, peering uneasily at the wrench in his clenched hand. Then Miller raised the wrench and went for them, and the younger moaned and ran. The older did not move. Miller, lowering his arm, stopped short. The boy's gaze was bared, implacable. Then he, too, turned and moved after the other, and took his hand. Miller watched until their small shimmering forms disappeared behind black boulders on the long road to Sonoita.

Swaying on the road, Miller licked his lips. Something had passed. Maybe the kid was only trying to help, he thought. What the hell's the matter? Didn't you see them children holding hands?

"You ignorant bastard," he murmured, stunned. He repeated it, then cried aloud in pain. He ran to the car and finished the job, leaving the tools and broken tire on the road. The motor started weakly, but in his desperate efforts to turn the car around, he sank it inexorably into the sand of the road shoulder. The engine block cracked and the car died. He got out and stared at what he had done, and then, because he could not stand his self-disgust, he started off, half-running, in the direction taken by the children.

Nearing the boulders, he stopped and shouted, *"Niños, niños! I don't mean no harm!"*

But his throat was parched and his tongue dry, and the sound he made was cracked and muted. Somewhere the boys were taking shelter, but if they heard him, they were afraid and silent. Over his head, the sun glowed like a great, white coal, dull with the ash of its own burning, without light.

"*Niños!*"

He knew now he would never find the children, but he also knew that if he did not find them, they might die; he could not go on without them. He got up tiredly and entered the maze of rocks, calling out every little while to the vast silence. The rocks climbed gradually in growing masses toward a far black butte, and as the day burned to its end, the wind died and a pallid sun shone through the haze. It sank away, and its last light crept slowly toward the summit, reddening the stones to fierce magnificence, only to fade at sunset into the towering sky.

Miller toiled up through the shadows. He reached the crest toward evening, on his knees, and his movement ceased. From somewhere below, a little later, he heard a shrill, clear call, and the call was answered, as he awoke, from a point nearer. In the dream, the children had walked toward him hand in hand.

He sat up a little, blinking, and fingered the dry furrows of his throat. To the north, the body of the flyer kept him company, its unclosed eyes outraged, uncomprehending. But Miller, without thinking, understood. His hand fell and, as his wait began, his still face grew entranced, impassive. The rocks turned cold. About him, in strange shapes of night, the mountains of Mexico gaped, crowded, leapt and stretched away across the moonlit wastes. The nameless range where he now lay stalked south through the Gran Desierto, sinking at last on the dead, salt shores of the Gulf of California.

Harper's Bazaar
August 1958

93010159